Hostage to Death

He had the kind of sharp, vivid imagination which could be both visionary and practical and he now stared at the suitcase and let his mind run riot. The police and Wraight had assumed that the strong-room had been left in a shambles as an act of bloody-minded vandalism. But suppose the real reason was to make certain that for several hours no one could check whether anything were missing? A lot of money, in the higher denomination notes, could be stuffed into a large suitcase. That suitcase could be renamed, lashed up and sealed with the bank seal (kept in the wooden box). When someone came to withdraw the suitcase (one gunman had escaped — because he had to organize the withdrawal, not for the far more obvious reason that he wished to be free?) and the police asked him if it was in order, he'd point to the unbroken seals. He'd be able to walk out of the bank without a moment's suspicion touching him. . . .

He stared at the suitcase.

JEFFREY ASHFORD

Hostage to Death

WALKER AND COMPANY · NEW YORK

First published in the United States of America in 1977 by the
Walker Publishing Company, Inc.

This paperback edition first published in 1985.

ISBN: 0-8027-3102-3

Library of Congress Catalog Card Number: 77-80204

Printed in the United States of America

10   9   8   7   6   5   4   3   2   1

Hostage
to
Death

Other titles in the Walker British Mystery Series

I

The bank, which was situated in the high street at the point at which the road began to dip towards the traffic lights, had been ringed by policemen. Six of them were armed with revolvers and six with rifles equipped with telescopic sights. The buildings on either side of the bank, and the flat above it, had been evacuated and were now occupied by police. To the rear of the bank, and protecting it from the road, was a courtyard and a ten-foot-high brick wall in which were tall wooden doors. Against the wall a scaffolding platform had been erected and from this the police kept watch. Three patrol cars were parked in the high street and of these one was used as a communications centre and another as a place where senior police officers could briefly rest or hold conferences which ran no risk of being overheard.

The public – and even late at night they were there in numbers – were held back in a flattened semi-circle whose radius was three hundred yards from the bank's outside doors. The two TV teams had taken all their stock shots and now the crews sat around and played poker and waited, hopefully, for a crisis.

At the police's orders the water company had cut off all water to the bank. The Post Office had rigged up a telephone in the patrol car which was being used as a communications centre.

Relatives of the hostages were allowed to watch from

5

the point where the right-hand semi-circle of onlookers became flattened and cut off by the row of shops on the opposite side of the road. There was always either a detective or a uniform sergeant present to comfort them and assure them that no harm had or would come to anyone and to suggest they went home to wait since they would be called out the moment anything happened. Few took the good advice. The remainder, tired, frightened, stared at the wooden doors, with the bank's crest on them, or the three tall windows, and despairingly wondered what was happening behind these.

     .   .   .   .

All it had taken had been one lousy scream, thought Val Thomas with renewed bitterness. He reached into his pocket and brought out a pack of cigarettes which he'd taken from one of the bank staff. He lit a cigarette. Originally his orders had been no smoking because a butt could tell a split a story, but that precaution was now a waste of time.

One lousy scream, he thought yet again, as he drew on the cigarette which rubbed against the edge of the mouth-hole in his nylon hood. The woman clerk had screamed and all five of them had swung round to check who was the nearest to shut her up: in that second someone had pressed a hidden panic button. He didn't know which of the staff had been the clever bastard: had he known, he'd have smashed him.

He stared along the length of the bank. The staff and the customers who'd been in the bank when the raid began were sitting or lying down in front of the counter which ran the length of the main area. The men were beginning to look scrubby because of the stubble on their chins – except for the soft looking, bespectacled clerk whose chin still looked smooth. A poof, thought Thomas with contempt. 'We'll shoot 'em, one at a time, if you don't lay on escape cars,' he'd told the split over the telephone. He'd knock off that fairy first. But he remembered the police's reply: 'No matter what happens, we won't release you. Kill anyone and your situation will be far worse.' If they left the hostages alone they'd collect a stiff sentence, but one with an end to it: kill any of the hostages and if the police didn't give way then they'd collect life and it would be life. Their strength had become their weakness.

Could the police refuse to negotiate and continue to put the lives of all the hostages at risk? Had they the moral strength to stand out against the emotional pressures raised by the threat to kill the hostages? He wanted to think the hadn't, but they'd recently broken several hostage sieges by refusing to trade, no matter what the cost.

His mind veered round to optimism. One dead man could make a whole world of difference (the British could be very sentimental). So suppose he blasted that poof into hell and had his corpse flung out on to the pavement in front of the public and the TV? Then the emotional pressures would boil. His optimism waned. If the police hung on and refused to give way despite the death, or deaths, then eventually it would be a murder rap for them all and the judge would hand down a sentence that would make topping a soft way out. After ten years in the stir, a man went soft: stir-fever. Prison life became normal, outside life abnormal.

He dropped the cigarette on to the floor and ground it out with the heel of his shoe, picked up the sawn-off shotgun which he had put down on the till counter. He walked down to the 'Foreign Business' counter. He'd like a ticket to somewhere else, bloody quickly, he thought with mordant humour. Next to this counter was a two-foot-six swing door which gave access to the passage beyond. He leaned over the door and released the retaining catch, pushed the door inwards, and passed through. To the left of the open passage were several doors: assistant manager's office, male and female cloakrooms, store-room and, at the far end and at right angles to the others, the door to the strong-room.

He opened the end door and went down the concrete stairs. The large basement was divided into two by the strong-room whose reinforced concrete wall, with sensor alarms set in it, was twelve feet from the foot of the stairs. The door into the strong-room was circular, eighteen inches thick at its thickest, and made from layers of different metals to increase its strength and bleed away heat: on the outside was the large wheel which operated the manual locking lugs and the time clock which set the electrically controlled locking lugs. The surround was metal two feet deep, bonded to the concrete with specially strengthened tie rods, with lug holes at regular intervals.

Ginger Chase sat on the table, heaped up with bundles of bank notes, in the first part of the strong-room. He looked up. 'What's happening now?'

'Nothing,' replied Thomas as he stepped over the circular sill into the strong-room. 'They're still outside and we're still inside.' He walked past the table. The further half of the strong-room was taken up with shelves, three feet high, on which were stored customers' valuables. The shelves ran round three walls and then came out on either side for five feet to leave an open doorway of six feet. He went through this open doorway and stood in the centre of the area and stared round at the shelves. On them were suitcases, in every shape and colour, wooden and cardboard boxes, tea chests, strong-boxes, and packing cases, many of them lashed with twine whose knots were sealed with sealing-wax. There could be half a dozen fortunes in them, he thought. Gold, platinum, silver, diamonds, rubies, sapphires, emeralds, pearls. . . .

Chase had slid off the table and now he came to the open doorway. 'So nothing's happening. We're here and they're there. So how long do we sit around?'

Chase had removed his nylon hood and Thomas stared at his heavily featured, powerful face. 'Until they change their minds.'

'And you reckon they're going to?'

'I reckon.'

Chase scowled his angry disagreement. He turned and went back to the table with the money on it. For some reason which he'd either never fully understood himself or else had been unwilling to explain – it couldn't have been fear – he'd been against the bank raid as planned from the beginning.

He picked up a thick bundle of new notes, bound by a brown paper wrapper. 'Twenties,' he said in his hoarse, croaky voice which made it sound as if he suffered from a permanent sore throat. He waved the bundle in the air. 'Fifty thousand quids' worth of twenties – all bloody wastepaper.' He threw the notes on to the table.

Soon after the siege had begun, Thomas had come down into the strong-room and emptied the bundles of notes, each in a leadfoil container, out of the green canvas sacks, padlocked and sealed, in which they had been brought to the bank. He knew the numbers off by heart. Two large bundles of twenties and one small – a hundred and twenty thousand pounds: five bundles of tens – a hundred and twenty-five thousand pounds: ten bundles of fives – two hundred and fifty thousand pounds: twenty large bundles of ones – a hundred thousand pounds. Five hundred and ninety-five thousand pounds in new notes. Probably something over three hundredweights of money. Add to that the old notes and the customers' valuables. . . . They were millionaires. Yet one lousy scream had made certain that they were millionaires only whilst they stayed inside and the police outside.

.   .   .   .   .

His parents hadn't been very wide awake or they would never have christened him Cyril. C. Rook. It was not a very good name for a detective inspector. To an outsider the joke was rather a thin one, but inside the force it continued to amuse long after it should have been pensioned off. If his character had been different, perhaps it would have been.

He was a good detective who managed to annoy both his superiors and his inferiors by his insistence on observing the rules, even when everyone else knew that there were times when they needed to be studied with Nelson's blind eye. It wasn't really any lack of imagination or initiative, but just his refusal to set even one foot out on a limb. If one stayed within the rules, one must be covered. In many ways it was strange that someone so careful should have joined the police force.

In physical appearance he was a stand-in for Mr Average Man. He was of average height, average build, and was neither good-looking nor ugly. His eyes were an ordinary shade of brown and his eyebrows didn't arch or droop. His brown hair wasn't greying and if it were beginning to thin this fact wasn't yet obvious. His nose was regular, his mouth precise, and his lips suggested a well-balanced libido. When he smiled, which wasn't all that often, there was usually a sense of reserve to that smile. He dressed as well as he could afford, which wasn't very well, and he liked a clean shirt every day.

'Shall I try to raise them again, sir?' he asked.

Pollock, assistant chief constable, looked briefly at Rook, then back at the bank. 'You might as well, mightn't you?'

'Right, sir. I'll go and try.' Rook was always very careful to call his seniors 'sir' as often as was reasonable. This was not from any sense of servility but because he believed one must always pay the proper respect to rank. In a hazy fashion he understood that his kind of world depended on due respect being paid to rank and that was why he disliked the modern protestors, whether of the right or left.

Rook crossed to the white patrol car which was their command centre. A TV camera tracked him. It was the first time he'd handled a case which hit the national headlines and he couldn't really reconcile himself to the attendant publicity. Would Amy laugh when she saw him on the TV?

Detective Sergeant Young, who sat in the front seat of the car with the door open, said: 'Is anything moving yet?'

Young more often than not didn't bother with a 'Sir'. It irritated Rook, though he never pulled rank on it. 'Nothing's altered so I'm going to try and talk to them again.'

'Keep the dialogue going, no matter what the reception?' Young grinned.

Rook recognized the words as a quote from the latest pamphlet, drawn up by H.Q., 'Procedure on hostage-related cases'. He'd read it through very carefully a month ago, memorizing all the relevant points.

He opened the back door and sat down. The telephone had been put on the back parcels shelf and he lifted off the receiver and dialled. The ringing began.

'Yeah?' said a voice which sounded harsh.

'This is Detective Inspector Rook.'

'Don't you ever sleep?'

'You haven't been giving me much of a chance . . . I want to know if there's anything you'd like us to send in to you and the hostages?'

'Bloody big deal!' Thomas could not hide his surprise – until now, the police had refused to provide anything.

'We could send in food and water.' The pamphlet from H.Q. had clearly laid down the various stages. 'After cutting their communications and for a reasonable length of time denying them any request, so bringing home to them their complete loneliness, offer them a few basic necessities (this will, in any case, have to be done out of consideration for the hostages). In this way a rapport will be built up between police and captors which can be utilized to persuade the captors that only the police are offering them any sympathy and understanding. . . .' It was the age-old cat-and-mouse game: the hard-and-soft pitch. Kick a man really hard and he'll be grateful if next time you kick him only softly.

Thomas tried to reassert his authority. 'Listen – there's only two hours before we hit the first hostage.'

This was the fourth different deadline the police had been given. Rook spoke as he might have done to a child and his pedantic authority made his words effective. 'Let's forget all that sort of nonsense. We both know you're not going to be stupid enough to actually kill when we've got you surrounded and you've no way out. You're not going to buy yourself a murder rap.'

Thomas stubbornly repeated the threat. 'In two hours we're hitting the first hostage unless you lay on cars and then a plane to take us and six hostages out of the country.'

'You're not going anywhere and you know it.'

'You've only two hours.'

'How d'you feel about some grub? There's a restaurant along the road that'll lay it on. What's more, you're lucky – it'll come for free.'

'Stuff the grub.'

'Surely the ladies are getting hungry and thirsty? Give me a bit of time to organize things and I'll get a couple of coppers to drop the grub and some water on the steps in front of the doors. How's that sound?'

Thomas hesitated for a long time, then said: 'One quick move from either of 'em and we'll hit the first hostage.'

'I'll send in the slowest moving couple I can find.' It was the breakthrough, thought Rook with gratification, but no surprise since the pamphlet from H.Q. had foretold exactly how events would work out.

2

Bill Steen eased his weight from one buttock to the other and leaned his right shoulder against the wooden wall of the counter. One of the hooded gunmen watched him, his ugly, truncated shotgun cradled in his right arm so that it could be instantly flipped up to bear on a target. Initially, Steen's mind had been filled with fearful thoughts of his head being shattered by a charge from one of the guns, but familiarity bred if not contempt then limited acceptance even towards his own murder and for many hours his desperate worry had been Penny.

With her, shock or tension often brought on a sudden attack of asthma so what would have happened when she'd learned about the bank raid and his being taken as one of the hostages, under threat of death? He was convinced she must have suffered an attack. The torturing question was, how serious an attack? A relatively mild one, capable of being contained by pills? A mediumly serious one, necessitating an injection of adrenalin? Or a severe one, so that she had to go to hospital, suddenly hollow-faced, struggling for breath until in an oxygen tent?

Asthma, he'd once read, had never killed anyone. Maybe. But its side and after effects had killed with profligate freedom. Emphysema, strained heart, grossly lowered resistance to other diseases ...

After the third serious attack in the first five months of their marriage he'd said to their G.P.: 'I can't understand why it's got so much worse since we married.'

The G.P. — elderly and old-fashioned enough to be genuinely concerned in helping his patients — had spoken with tired defeat. 'We think we know a lot about asthma now — and we really know next to nothing. It comes without warning, it can disappear without reason. Any doctor can give you a list of probabilities and he can also tell you how often those probabilities turn out to be totally wrong. In your wife's case, her asthma is clearly both nervous and allergic in origin: somewhere along the line, her marriage has triggered off certain nervous signals.'

14

He'd said angrily: 'I don't beat her up every night.'

The doctor had smiled, sadly.

Her asthma had become worse. They'd gone to a specialist in London, a very well-dressed, urbane, sympathetic man.

'I'm afraid, Mr Steen, that it does happen in a few cases and we cannot really claim to understand the cause, although we can, of course, surmise that the tensions are subconscious and unrecognized. From what you have both told me there is no apparent reason for the worsening of Mrs Steen's asthma. Frankly I don't think that at the moment anything more can be done than to try somehow to discover what those tensions are, when steps can be taken to meet them, and to continue with your doctor's advice to take Intal up to four times a day and keep Ventolin handy since you have found that to be the most effective drug.'

'There must be something more?'

'From a practical viewpoint — I am afraid not.'

'Then from an impractical one?'

He'd rubbed his strong, square chin. 'Sometimes a complete change of environment can work what takes on the nature of a miracle. There's no real explanation of this in the case of nervous asthma, although with allergic asthma there may be an obvious one.'

'Does that mean that if we moved to another town she might be all right?'

'If your wife's asthma were purely allergic, a new part of the country might well offer relief: clay is a bad soil to live on, the country is filled with grass pollen at certain times of the year, the towns have air pollution. But since your wife's asthma is also nervously based, I was speaking in terms of another country where the whole tempo of life is totally different. Even taking a siesta with an easy conscience might bring relief.'

The interview had cost them twenty pounds. For a couple of days after it they'd talked about moving abroad and then the realities had swamped them. Their ties, their mortgaged house, and his job were all in England. Banking was not one of those jobs which made it easy to find employment in another country and in any case her mother was a permanent invalid and unless Penelope could be certain that she could quickly return to England in an emergency she could never happily live abroad whilst her mother was alive: and the specialist had made it clear that such a life would have to be happily lived if she were to benefit. . . .

A guard came along. He was well built, obviously strong, and moved with the easy rhythm of someone in good physical shape. He passed the captives without bothering to look at them and went up to the inside glass and wood doors which led into the six-foot-deep porch-like space before the outside wooden doors. He opened one of the glass and wood doors and pushed down the rubber stop to hold it open. The hostages watched, nervously trying to decide what his actions portended.

He unlocked and unbolted the wooden doors and pulled the right-hand one open. There was a rising hum of excitement from all the onlookers outside: TV cameras zoomed in, the police tensed and those with arms gripped them a shade more tightly.

He picked up the two metal containers that were on the top step immediately outside the door. He carried them through the porch and put them down, then returned to rebolt and relock the outside door.

Abrahams, who lay a dozen people along from Steen, said loudly: 'That's got to be something to eat.'

Hodges, next to him, said: 'But not for you – you're on a diet.'

Someone laughed because Abrahams's diet was a standing joke ('And it stands sixteen stone on its twelve-size feet').

Steen was surprised to discover how some of the fear and tension had been lifted from the situation, even though the threat to their lives had become no less.

.   .   .   .   .

It was night. Around the front of the bank were nine portable arc lamps, set in a semi-circle to supplement the street lighting: the brickwork looked shabby in such stark light, instead of mellow and soft-toned.

Rook stifled his yawn.

'Go and put your head down for a couple of hours,' said Detective Superintendent Mellon.

'It's all right, thanks, sir.'

'We'll try and get along without you.' Mellon grinned.

They did not like each other, but Rook worked very hard to hide the fact. Mellon was large in build and expansive in character. He had an easy, friendly manner which usually concealed the fact that he also had a sharp temper. At work he called for results and did not, unless necessary, enquire into how those had been obtained.

Rook tried not to yawn again and ended up watery-eyed and swallowing hard.

'For God's sake, man, go away and put your head down somewhere.'

Now it was an order, not a suggestion. 'I'll go to the station, sir. If anything happens here while I'm away . . .'

'We'll call for the fire brigade.'

Rook attempted to smile, but wasn't very successful.

17

He was always being caught between his disapproval of the inanities of life and the need to hide his disapproval when it was his seniors who perpetrated them.

He turned and walked away to his right. He passed several shops to come to the point where a uniform constable was keeping a narrow path free through the watching crowds. As he approached the gap a sloppily dressed, long-haired man called out: 'Hey, Inspector, what's fresh?' He identified the man as belonging to one of the TV teams. He stopped. 'There's no change in the situation.'

'Are you sending more grub inside?'

'If that becomes necessary.'

'D'you know for certain how many gunmen there are?'

'No,' He resumed walking to go through the gap.

The TV reporter had dodged through the crowd. 'Come on, unbutton. Give me something fresh to gnaw on.'

'The situation has in no way altered since the last press conference.'

'How can I turn that into news?' the reporter grumbled as he dropped back.

In fact, Rook thought with tired satisfaction, the situation had changed a great deal -- the worst was over and had been from the moment the wooden doors had opened and the hooded man had come out to pick up the two containers. Now, it was only a question of time. The gunmen would become more and more dependent on the police and less and less able to carry out their threats of murder, because the bonds of a shared ordeal would emotionally bind closer together captors and captives. It had been a textbook -- or H.Q. pamphlet -- operation.

He turned right at the cross-roads and went down Station Road. For him, this case was proving to be a slice of luck. When the gunmen filed out of the bank and threw down their guns to surrender, not even Mellon would be able to deny him his success. Next year there was going to be a vacancy at H.Q. for an administrative detective chief inspector and that was a job tailored for him.

He again turned to the right to pass a building site which only six months before had been the large front garden of the vicarage, and crossed the road to the ten storey, glass and concrete divisional H.Q., which four years before had replaced the then totally inadequate and ramshackle old H.Q.

Young, looking quite fresh, was in Rook's room, talking over the telephone. He stood up and, still talking, moved round to sit on the edge of the desk. Rook, now that he was out of sight of the public, took off his coat to show he wore braces and sat down.

Young finally replaced the receiver. 'Eastcote's just rung in. They've picked up a couple of youngsters who broke into a house in their territory.'

'Have they . . . ?'

'Not to fuss, Chief. Everything's in order.'

'I've told you before, don't call me that,' he snapped.

Young grinned as he stood up. 'Well, I'll be off and leave you to yourself.'

Rook watched Young leave. Far too big for his boots. One day he'd trip over them and fall flat on his face. People who breezed through life always came a cropper in the end.

He told the duty sergeant to call him in two hours and then slumped down in the chair and closed his eyes. Perhaps he ought to have rung Amy just to say he was O.K., but he was so tired, it was very late, and in any case she probably wasn't worrying. Early in their marriage he'd unexpectedly been held up for hours and unable to contact her and when he'd finally returned home he'd thought to find her worried sick for his safety. She'd been so unperturbed that he'd become quite annoyed . . . Much to her kind amusement.

He cleared his mind for the sleep he so desperately needed and perversely it refused to come.

. . . .

Thomas belched. He stared at the hostages, stretched along the floor as they tried to sleep, and that belch was a sign of the contempt he felt for them.

He pulled out a cigarette from the pack and since this was the last he crumpled up the pack and dropped it on to the floor. He lit the cigarette and smoked. Only a day and a half ago it had all looked so certain: a quick snatch, following weeks of surveillance, and enough money to make them all rich. But a woman had given one lousy scream . . .

There had to be some way out. . . . Suppose they sliced off an ear from one of the hostages and slung that out of the bank and said that that was for starters? Mightn't that stoke up public concern even more than a death?

After an attempted armed robbery, without violence actually being used, the sentence was likely to be fifteen years. With full remission that would mean ten years in the nick. Ten years would take him over the hill.

He dropped the cigarette to the floor. He walked along to the swing door, pushed this open, and continued to the manager's office, which he entered. He sat down behind the desk and thought with contempt that it wasn't much of an office to set on top of millions of pounds.

How to escape the inescapable? He sat back in the

chair, which tilted to accommodate the new angle of his body. There must be some way out. . . . But how could you get past an army of coppers?

．   ．   ．   ．

Steen awoke as he turned. His left arm was numb because he'd been lying on it and he rubbed it as the pins-and-needles started pricking. He looked at his wristwatch. Four-nineteen. Was Penelope awake at that moment?

He remembered her last bad attack. Every time she caught a cold they worried, whilst they assured each other there was no need to worry, fearful that the cold would develop into bronchitis and the bronchitis would trigger off asthma. For two days their optimism had been rewarded. Then, at three the next morning, the bronchitis had started.

The doctor had prescribed antibiotics. Ironically, the antibiotics which for her acted most effectively were often the ones which had the worst side effects. 'Life's got a bloody warped sense of humour,' the doctor had once said. This time the antibiotic had had to be changed and immediately the bronchitis had become worse. He'd listened to her whistling, laboured breathing and had known the old familiar fear and impotent anger that anyone who had never harmed another should so have to suffer.

Asthma had arrived like a bomb and within twenty-four hours she had been white-faced, dull-eyed, coughing, and with heart thumping. The doctor had given her an injection of adrenalin which had helped, but only temporarily.

He'd driven her to hospital and an oxygen tent. As she lay inside the transparent plastic tent, the oxygen gently hissing, he'd held her hand and stared at her as he'd tried

21

to imprint in his mind every single one of her physical features because deep within him there had been the unspoken, unthought thought that this could be the last attack — that despite all her fighting courage she was going to prove wrong the medical aphorism that asthma never killed.

She'd returned home four days later, white-faced, drawn, weak, but smiling. And once again he'd wondered how much of her suffering had been due to marrying him and whether living abroad, no matter what the sacrifices, would really help.

His gloomy thoughts were interrupted by Gaitshead — a large, rugger-playing man — who lay next to him. 'So you're awake as well,' he said, in what he presumably thought was a whisper. 'By God, Bill, I could murder a pint! What d'you reckon the police would say if we asked 'em to send in some beer?'

Steen again looked at his watch. 'Sorry, it's after closing time.'

'Hilarious! . . . Imagine a pint of bitter.'

'Stop torturing yourself and think of women instead.'

'I've tried and they all look like bottles. It's that first swallow as it slides down the throat . . .'

'Can't you stop talking?' said Miss Tucker severely. 'Some of us are trying to sleep.'

'You're lucky you don't find the floor too hard,' replied Gaitshead.

It was unfortunate that Miss Tucker was on the plump-ish side.

3

The sunlight came at a low angle through the gap in the curtains to awaken Thomas. He was thick-headed and his mouth tasted like an uncollected dustbin. He stood up, brushed the palm of his hand over his head and then reluctantly pulled on the nylon hood. It was going to be another warm day and the hood quickly made his face prickle with sweat.

He walked round the desk to the window and pulled the curtains apart until he could look out. Two policemen's heads cleared the brick wall as they kept watch from the other side. Knock 'em down like targets in a slot machine, he thought with sharp hate. But shoot a copper and you didn't need to worry about what you'd do after you came out of the nick.

He returned to the desk and sat down on it. Ginger had been shouting his complaints and the others were becoming very restive, yet all of them still basically had enough faith in him to believe that he'd get them out of the trap. Couldn't they yet see that he'd begun to lose faith in himself?

Was he hanging on in the bank from pride, because he couldn't bear to turn his back on at least a million quid, or because he instinctively believed there was always a way out, however hopeless the situation looked? They were surrounded by the police who refused to give way before any pressure. Logically, then, they must give in. But to accept that was to accept defeat. Suddenly he realized that once he truly accepted the fact that there could be no escape then, and only then, was there a chance of escape for them.

The assistant chief constable stood facing the small semi-circle of senior officers: the chief superintendent from H.Q., the divisional superintendent, and the divisional chief inspector, were in uniform and looked smart, Mellon and Rook were in crumpled shirts and looked, with their stubbled chins, rather like tramps.

'All right, gentlemen,' Pollock concluded, 'that's quite clear, is it? We keep everything in very low key and carry on exactly as we have been?'

They nodded.

'Good.' Pollock nodded, turned, and walked towards the command patrol car.

Mellon turned to the left and Rook kept pace with him. 'I'll be glad when it's all over,' said Mellon. 'I'm getting too old to be up day and night.' He stopped and looked at the bank. 'Why can't they admit defeat and come on out? Then we could all go home and have a square meal and a bed to sleep on.'

'I suppose they're hoping against hope we'll break first.'

'I suppose.' Mellon now sounded bored by the conversation even though he had initiated it. He rubbed his thick, heavy chin which added the bulldog look to his features. 'What d'you imagine they're doing and thinking?'

Rook was not really surprised that Mellon should return to a subject he had a moment before apparently found boring: Mellon had the irritating habit of concealing the true direction of his thoughts and the kind of malicious sense of humour which gained amusement from someone else's subsequent confusion. 'The best estimate we can get is there's over half a million in new cash inside, apart from all the customers' valuables. They'll still be trying desperately to work out a way to escape with some or all of that half million even though it's obvious they can't.'

'Yeah.' This time, Mellon's tone of voice was thoughtful.

24

'They'll be twisting their brains dry for an answer. Killing the hostages is out, so what's left? A shoot-out? No one's caught sight of anything stronger than a sawn-off shotgun. However desperate, you don't have a shoot-out if you've only saw-offs and the opposition's got rifles. So what are they working on? There's no way out of the building except through the front or back door.'

'Could they be thinking of somehow using explosives?'

'Why should they have any with them? They hit the bank after it had opened to the public so that the strong-room should be open. They'd not have been expecting to blow anything.'

'Then maybe all they're trying to do is buy time because they reckon that when nothing happens for hour after hour we'll get bored and a lot less sharp.'

'It's your job to make certain every man is snap on the button,' said Mellon, as if he'd reason for supposing the D.I. had allowed slackness to creep in.

'Of course, sir,' said Rook stiffly. 'But I can guarantee that every man *is* doing his job. . . .'

'Relax.'

Rook suffered further resentment.

⋅⋅⋅⋅⋅⋅⋅⋅

'Do you know what the record for drinking beer is?' asked Gaitshead.

'Thankfully, no,' replied Steen.

'Guinness won't list it, but I was told it was twenty pints in the hour. When they let me out of here I'm heading for the nearest pub and I'm going to kick that miserable dribble straight down the plug-hole.'

If they were let out of the bank. Because he was both

a realist and a dreamer, Steen could judge how thin was the safety line behind which the hostages lived. The realist said that if the gunmen judged that the death of one or more hostages would gain them their freedom, they would kill. The dreamer saw himself as the chosen victim. The quick order, the few moments of shocked understanding, the split second when eternity was nearly now, and then the shot. . . .

The gunman who was clearly the leader walked the length of the bank and stopped by the right-hand window. He stared out at the street, his shoulders squared. Defying everyone, thought Steen, and became more frightened for his own and Penelope's sake because all the time the gunmen were defiant they must surely be considering the benefits of killing?

.　　.　　.　　.　　.

Thomas once again checked off the others in his mind. Ginger was too obvious, both in looks and character. Because he was so large a man with bright red hair he was remarkable in almost any company and if something annoyed him he was liable to react immediately and without thought. Alf Brent was far more self-controlled, but he had a very noticeable scar on his right cheek. Flash Jenkins would be too sure of himself. From the start he'd be so certain of success that he'd get careless. That left Paul Drude. Ordinary-looking – no hint of his vicious nature – controlled in manner, and reliable. As an added bonus he had a wife and two kids and the fear of what could happen them would keep him straight. But he was a bit slow to change his ideas to meet unexpected circumstances . . . He ought to choose himself, thought Thomas, but Ginger would immediately become suspicious. In any case, it was going to be very hard going to sell them the idea that solely by surrendering could they hope to escape – so only by staying with them would he persuade them to buy.

He turned. He studied the bank staff and momentarily grinned sardonically. With their stubbled chins, rumpled clothes, and unwashed faces and bodies, they looked the kind of people you wouldn't lend a torn quid.

He walked the length of the bank to the swing door and went along the open passage and down to the strong-room, now empty. One of the bundles of twenties – the large size, he judged, containing fifty thousand pounds – had been ripped open and the notes scattered about: it was odds on Ginger had stuffed a number of the notes into his pockets, knowing there was not the slightest hope of hiding them through any search, yet unable to resist the illusion of wealth.

He moved on, through the gap between the shelves, and stared at the collection of suitcases, boxes, strong-boxes, cartons, and tea chests. Roughly half of them must be ripped open and their contents scattered about. Then the remaining money must also be scattered everywhere so that it would take the staff hours to check out the total amounts. Until the final figures were calculated, the police would put the mess down to the childish resentment of villains who'd failed.

How much dare he try to get out initially? It must be the maximum whose bulk would not draw attention: twenties were out because banks still kept their numbers (inflation now prevented their keeping the numbers of lesser denominations) and so they could only be regarded in the light of a long-term investment.

Timing was all important and he decided to set H hour at twenty to ten – soon after the bank would normally have opened. He'd better start sounding like a beaten man so that their capitulation did not come so unexpectedly as to make someone wonder why. No one must wonder why until it was too late.

.   .   .   .   .

Rook stepped out of the patrol car to come face-to-face with Mellon.

'What do you want this time?' asked Mellon.

Rook spoke with quiet satisfaction. 'To know if we'll go easy with them if they give up peacefully.'

'So!' Mellon's round, tired face showed his satisfaction. 'I told 'em we'd guarantee nothing.'

'Of course.'

There was no 'Of course' about it, thought Rook with brief resentment. Some D.I.s would have half-promised help in return for an immediate surrender – but, as always, he had abided by the rules.

'How did he take your answer?'

'Swore and slammed down the receiver.'

Mellon nodded. That was the kind of initial reaction to be expected. He looked up at the cloudless sky. By this time tomorrow, he thought, it would quite possibly all be over.

4

Thomas sat on the edge of the table in the first part of the strong-room and stared at Drude. 'Whatever happens, play it cool.' He fidgeted with a bundle of ten-pound notes, running his thumbnail up and down the corners. If only he could do the job himself . . . 'Contact Dutch as soon as you're clear and if he's sober give him this signature – if he isn't sober, get a stomach pump.' He handed over a sheet of paper on which he had signed the name A. R. Parsons. 'And watch him, eh?'

'I'll watch him closer'n my own shadow, Val.'

Thomas stared at the hard, muscular figure of Drude, who wasn't wearing a hood. His face was regular and it only missed being handsome because it was a shade too long: it was not a face readily recalled when at the time there had been no reason to note it. In any case, the coppers' real worry would be the gunmen in the bank. 'Don't get any clever ideas afterwards,' he said softly.

Drude shrugged his shoulders. 'I'm not that big a mug.'

They both knew that but for his wife and children he would at least have been tempted. There'd be enough money to make even a saint think twice.

Thomas slid off the table. 'O.K. Let's have a check to make certain we can fix enough folding on to you.'

Drude, like the rest of them, was wearing new dark blue cotton shirt, dark blue jeans, plimsolls, socks, pants, and thin nylon gloves, all bought in multiple stores and untraceable. He pulled off his shirt to reveal a well-bronzed torso. He unzipped his trousers and slipped them off after removing the plimsolls.

Previously, Thomas had separated a bundle of two thousand five hundred ten-pound notes into five bundles of five hundred and these had been fitted into the pockets of a rough money-belt fashioned out of a length of linen towel from one of the cloakrooms. He tied the money-belt around Drude's waist, stepped back, and examined it critically. 'Get dressed.'

When Drude was dressed it was possible to make out the uneven bulge around his waist, but Thomas was satisfied that no one would casually remark it. 'Try moving about.'

Drude walked round the table, bent down, twisting his body to the right and left. Thomas heard no rustling of paper. 'You'll go through as easy as a dose of salts,' he said, feeling almost as confident as he sounded.

'Who are you going to take for clothes, Val?'

'There's two blokes look to be your size: we'll try one of them.'

'I'd give a lot to be around to see the splits' faces.'

If he was around, thought Thomas, he'd get his bloody neck broken.

.   .   .   .   .

It had just turned dark when Thomas came up to the line of hostages, stopped in front of a man, and said: 'You – get up.' He then indicated the two men on either side. 'And you two.'

They hesitated.

'Get on your feet,' he ordered roughly.

Aspinall was the first to rise. He was in early middle age and had the slack flesh of someone who ate a little too much and seldom took exercise. 'What . . . what's the matter?' he asked hoarsely.

30

Thomas ignored him, suddenly went forward and booted Cantor in the side. Cantor cried out, as much from the shock as the pain. Deeding, the third man, hurriedly scrambled to his feet.

'Get along to the manager's office,' said Thomas.

As soon as Cantor was standing, a hand pressed to his side, they went along to the swing door.

Watching them, Steen wondered if he would ever see them again. Thank God, he thought ashamedly, that he had not been chosen.

.   .   .   .   .

A uniform P.C. hurried up to where Rook stood. 'P.C. Shrewsbury reports three men have been taken under armed guard into the manager's office, sir.'

Rook swung round and stared at the front of the bank, once more harshly outlined by the arc lamps.

There was a shout. 'Telephone.'

He ran the twenty yards to the patrol car, climbed in the back and lifted the receiver as a cycle of ringing ended. 'This is Detective Inspector . . .'

'I've got three blokes all ready. Get the cars or I'm taking 'em one after the other.' The connexion was cut.

He dialled the bank's number and the ringing began, but the call remained unanswered. He held the receiver close by his left ear as he leaned out of the opened door-way. 'Call Mr Mellon.'

Mellon had been close to the car and he came over. 'What's the panic, then?'

'They've just been on the phone, sir. They've picked out three hostages and taken 'em through to the manager's office. They're threatening to kill 'em, one after the other.

I didn't get a chance to talk and I'm still trying to get back.'

Mellon stared at Rook for several seconds, then put his hands in his trousers pockets and began to jingle the coins in them. His expression which had sharpened began to relax. 'They're trying one last time to break our nerve.'

Rook was worried that Mellon could be quite so confidently certain. 'You don't think that it's just possible. . . ?'

'Not them. They can see the odds just as clearly as us. But they've nothing to lose by a final try.'

Neither of them realized that something concrete had been gained – a strengthening in the police's belief that the bank robbers were close to giving up.

.   .   .   .   .

The strong-room was now an Aladdin's cave of riches. All the green canvas bags had been emptied and notes were scattered everywhere. In the far half strong-boxes, boxes, suitcases, cartons, tea-chests, had been smashed open and their contents piled higgledy-piggledy all over the floor and shelving: there was a confusion of documents, silver teapots, coffee-pots, jugs, candelabra, sauceboats, epergnes, cutlery, of paintings, of incunabula, of porcelain, of necklaces, rings, brooches, tiaras, in gold, silver, platinum, pearls, sapphires, emeralds, diamonds, rubies . . .

Chase, who'd helped Thomas set the scene, swore with violent anger. A silver tankard, crested and inscribed, had spilled out into the front part of the strong-room. He kicked it and it hit the wall with a metallic ringing and dropped to the floor on to a loose heap of notes. He longed to destroy all this wealth rather than leave it behind.

'Let's get back up,' said Thomas.

Chase moved forward and reached past the shelves to

pick up a diamond necklace. The setting was heavy and the diamonds were large. 'What's it worth – ten grand?'

'More like twenty. Throw it back.'

He hurled it back.

Thomas checked the time. Nine o'clock. Three-quarters of an hour before they surrendered. If things worked out they wouldn't end up with the fortune they could have had, but they wouldn't starve and they'd have made the coppers look a bunch of ripe Charlies.

'It could've been the biggest job ever,' said Chase.

'Let's get up top.'

Thomas led the way out of the strong-room, across to the stairs, up to the main part of the bank and into the manager's office. The electric light was on because the curtains were drawn.

Brent sat behind the desk and on the desk was his sawn-off shotgun, the truncated muzzles pointing in the direction of the three bank staff who sat slumped against the far wall. They were ashen-faced, frightened sick by the long wait which must, they believed, end in their death.

Thomas jerked his thumb at Deeding. 'You – get up on your feet.'

Deeding began to shiver. He looked vainly at his companions as if expecting help from them, then struggled to his feet. 'Please, I . . .'

'Get through to the next room.' Thomas crossed to the second doorway which gave direct access into the assistant manager's office. He pulled the door open. When Deeding failed to move, he grabbed his right arm and forced him along. Deeding groaned. Contemptuously, Thomas shoved to send him spinning forward to crash into the desk. Thomas kicked the door shut with his feet. 'Strip off.'

'You can't do it. I've a wife. And two children . . .'

33

'Poor sods! Strip quick and maybe you'll see 'em again.'

Deeding stared at him, hope battling with fear, then with desperately clumsy fingers he removed his shoes, unbuttoned his coat, unzipped his trousers and took off both garments.

'And the rest, except for your pants.'

He removed shirt, tie, and socks.

'Lie down on the floor, on your stomach.'

He lay down and the sweat suddenly ran down from his armpits. Thomas brought his arms up behind his back, crossed the wrists and bound them together with adhesive tape, secured the ankles in the same way. He picked up the clothes, rolled them into a bundle, and took them out through the door which led into the open passage. Drude was waiting and followed him down to the strong-room.

As Drude undressed, Thomas picked up the money-belt and checked that the five bundles of notes were still secure. Drude took the belt and tied it around his waist, then dressed in Deeding's clothes. 'The shoes bloody pinch my toes,' he complained.

'If that's all that gets pinched, our luck's in.' Thomas studied him. Drude looked suitably shabby, since the suit was not a good fit, and suitably seedy, since his face was heavily stubbled. Would anyone begin to suspect he was not one of the hostages?

    •   •   •   •   •

Rook yawned three times in quick succession. God, he was tired! If he put his head down now he'd sleep for a week. He stared across the road at the bank, looking pleasantly mellow in the morning sunshine.

Mellon crossed over. 'They've got to end it soon,' he said, in tones of annoyance.

He was worrying, thought Rook with satisfaction. No longer the omniscient, he was beginning to think he might be wrong and that the gang weren't busted. No doubt he was remembering those three men who'd been moved into the manager's office the previous night . . .

Mellon checked his watch. 'Ring 'em up and . . .' He stopped. At this stage it had to be bad psychology to contact the gunmen. He dropped his left arm and looked at the bank. The mob, and in particular their leader, must be courageous, brutal, and to a degree, gamblers. His judgement had been that since yesterday they had accepted the inevitability of final defeat. Yet why had those three men been separated from the rest? Was it a last courageous, brutal gamble – yet to be played – to try to stave off the inevitable? A gamble already played and failed? A . . .

There was a loud call. 'All the hostages are being forced to their feet.'

Mellon and Rook tensed. Behind them in the buildings police marksmen stared through their telescopic sights at the windows and doors.

'This is it, Cyril,' said Mellon softly, now quite certain once more.

. . . . . .

Steen stood next to Miss Tucker and noticed that she smelled. Wryly, he decided she was almost certainly making the same discovery about him.

The gunman who was giving the orders approached the hostages, his sawn-off shotgun in the trail position and the twin muzzles pointing at them.

35

'Hasn't anyone ever told him how to hold a gun safely?' asked Gaitshead.

It was a good question, thought Steen.

'Move to the doors,' ordered the gunman.

The hostages shuffled forward, still uncertain, then the vision of freedom gripped them all and many began to push and shove to try to be the first out.

Wraight called out: 'Steady there. Come on, now, gentlemen, let's have some order. Ladies first.' His voice was high-pitched, his choice of words primly old-fashioned, yet people immediately behaved in a more controlled fashion.

The inner doors were pulled back and the stops pressed down to hold them open. The outer wooden doors were unbolted, unlocked, and opened. Immediately, the on-lookers began to call out and, as the first hostage stepped into full view, there were shouts.

Steen, towards the back of the queue, stepped down on to the pavement and into the sunshine. He eagerly looked around. He saw the crowds, the uniform P.C.s who controlled them, two dog handlers whose dogs sat by their sides, the patrol cars, and the group of policemen who were walking towards them, but there was no sign of Penelope.

A policeman raised a loudhailer. 'Will you all come this way: everyone this way, please.'

They were ushered into a shoe shop and a uniform inspector said that the moment they'd been seen by the doctor and had given their names and addresses to the sergeant they could go home. He hoped they'd have a peaceful rest of the day at home.

'Go home?' said Gaitshead loudly. 'Let's get the priorities right. Are the pubs open yet?'

Steen noted that he was the thirteenth person to go

into the manager's office to see the doctor. He wasn't normally superstitious, but he found himself hoping that this wasn't an augury.

The doctor was young and – perhaps understandably – somewhat brusque. 'Sit down over there. Your name is . . . ? Well, Mr Steen, how are you feeling? Have you suffered any hurt during your imprisonment?'

He was feeling emotionally drained, dead tired, and on edge with worry, but obviously the doctor was only interested in more particular complaints. 'I'm fine, thanks.'

'Good. I'll just give you a very quick check-up and first of all we'll have a look at your reactions. . . .'

He was passed fit. The doctor, as he wrote rapidly on a form, said: 'Get in touch with your own G.P. immediately if you have any cause. There might be some delayed shock.'

He left the office. A sergeant, with opened notebook in his right hand, came up and asked him for his name and address. 'We'll try not to bother you, sir, but once we get inside the bank we may find we'll need your help. If we do telephone you, please come back into town as soon as you can.'

'Of course,' he answered, with total insincerity. The first thing he'd do after greeting Penelope would be to take the receiver off its stand.

A reporter tried to question him, but he side-stepped the man. He went the length of the shop and out through the back door, which opened on to the large council car-park. He saw his car and began to run.

．　　　．　　　．　　　．　　　．

The assistant chief constable, the chief superintendent from H.Q., the divisional superintendent, Mellon, and

37

Rook, stood in front of the patrol cars. To the right, ten P.C.s and two sergeants waited in a tight group, ready to storm forward. In the windows and doorways of the shops and flats behind, armed marksmen maintained their aims.

'What in the name of hell are they waiting for?' murmured the assistant chief constable, his voice taut.

It was a perplexing question. With all the hostages released, the mob had left themselves powerless. What could they hope to gain by hanging on?

A uniform sergeant approached the group and made it clear that he wanted to speak to Rook. Rook moved over.

'The doctor's seen twenty-one hostages, sir, and they're all passed fit enough to go home. We've taken their names, addresses, and telephone numbers, and warned the staff members we may have to call them back at short notice.'

'Twenty-one?' said Rook, his mind more concerned with what the mob were doing in the bank than with what the sergeant was saying.

'The twenty-second bloke never bothered to see the doctor. We checked with the manager, because this bloke's one of the staff, and his name's Deeding.'

Rook shrugged his shoulders. It seemed of small moment that one of the staff should rush back to his family rather than wait for a medical check-up. He turned and went back to the group of senior officers.

A man with a hood over his head and a gun in the crook of his arm came into sight in the porch of the bank. The crowd became excited and the TV cameras zoomed in. Three more masked men, each with a gun on his arm, joined the first one and the police were suddenly afraid that, against all the logical odds, it was going to be a shoot-out after all.

In rough unison the gunmen moved out of the porch

38

on to the first step. They threw down their guns on to the pavement, then stood with hands on hips, proudly defiant in their defeat.

'Where's the fifth one?' said Mellon tightly.

5

As he drew level with the end of the old orchard which bordered their land, Steen saw the red-grey peg-tile roof of Tudor Cottage. It was a pretentious name since the house was no more than two hundred years old, but Penelope had refused to change it because of her love of the absurd. It was these odd quirks in her nature which so attracted him. Even after three years of marriage he could never be certain how she would react to a new situation.

He braked and turned right into the drive – they always called it 'the drive' for the same reason that the house remained Tudor Cottage – and stopped in front of the garage. He climbed out of the car. She'll come into view around the thorn hedge any second now, he thought. But no one appeared. He walked to the gate in the hedge, now knowing she could not be at home and yet still trying to imagine what was keeping her. He opened the gate, which as always squeaked, walked along the brick path around the corner of the kitchen and up to the porch.

Inside the porch, on the tile sill under the window, was

a folded sheet of paper, held down by a stone. Mrs Pledge, a near neighbour who had been a nurse, wrote that Penelope had had to go into hospital the previous day because of a sharp attack of asthma.

.   .   .   .   .   .

Once they were in the bank and had released the mentally exhausted but physically unharmed Deeding the police were able to reconstruct what had happened. One of the gunmen had dressed in Deeding's clothes and as the hostages crowded out of the bank had joined them. At such an emotional moment none of the hostages had noticed that there was a newcomer with them as they crossed the road. In the shoe shop there had been near turmoil, with hostages frantic to get away, the press asking questions, the TV teams snarling up all movement, and relations trying to speak to their kin: the gunman could have chosen almost any moment to leave unobserved.

Mellon, his face set in sharp, angry lines, stood in the bank in front of one of the cashier's points and said: 'Why weren't they counted. We knew there were twenty-two hostages.'

'Twenty-two people came out of the bank, sir,' said Rook tightly.

'I'm talking about the number who saw the doctor. If we'd known there was one short there we could've moved much earlier and grabbed the man.

Rook understood two things. Mellon had already heard about the report the sergeant had made concerning the number of people who had seen the doctor and he was going to use Rook's failure to inform him at the time of the known discrepancy to shift as much of the blame as he could on to Rook's shoulders, despite the fact that it was a hundred to one he would not immediately have understood the significance of the missing man.

. . . . . .

Penelope was in a bed at the far end of the ward. Because it was so sunny a day and the ward had large picture windows, curtains had been partially drawn to leave the patients in shade and this aggravated the wanness of her face: there were dark smudges under her blue eyes, which themselves were dull.

She gripped Steen's hand. 'Bill. Oh, Bill! . . . Are you all right?'

'Never felt better.' He stared down at her and noticed how she was still having to fight for each breath. 'But how are you?'

'Feeling very stupid and useless. Of all the times to get lumbered!'

He sat down on the plain wooden chair, still holding her hand. 'Has it been a bad attack, darling?'

'It had its moments, but it's all over and done with now. Mary was wonderful and looked after me at home because I so wanted to be there for when you got back, but in the end she wouldn't take the responsibility any longer and called Dr Bates. He gave me hell for not getting him before and sent me in here.'

It must have been a very sharp attack. Without realizing it, he tightened his grip.

She gazed up and visually searched his face. 'Are you sure you're really all right? You're not lying to keep me from worrying?'

'I'm tired, but that's all – considering we had to try to sleep on the floor, that's not surprising. And I'm hungry.

They sent in sandwiches – the person who originally made them has probably since died from old age.'

'And I'm not at home to cook you a really lovely meal. Damn my stupid body. Why . . .'

He leaned over and kissed her. 'I'll take a rain check on smoked salmon, coq au vin, a bottle of Château Margaux, Saint Honoré, and Tia Maria with whipped cream.'

She smiled. 'You'll be lucky! . . . Bill, what did you do all the time you were in the bank? It seemed a couple of ages and I kept wondering what you were doing.'

'At first we were all . . . shocked, I suppose is the word. Then when we got over that we just lay about on the floor and tried to sleep or find some other way of making time pass. I had Alan Gaitshead next to me so I had to listen to how much beer he was going to drink when he got the chance.'

'That must have been fun!'

'I could cheerfully have brained him – if that's possible. The more he went on, the thirstier I got.'

A nurse came up to the bed. 'I'm sorry, Mr Steen, but you'll have to leave.'

'But I've only just arrived,' he protested.

'I know, but it's not visiting hours and Mrs Steen must rest. You can come and see her again this evening.'

'Go along, Bill,' said Penelope, giving his hand a slight push as she released it. 'Now I know for certain you're O.K., I'll get better every minute. And the moment I'm home I'm going to cook you as much of that meal as housekeeping will run to.'

He smiled. 'A kipper, a roast broiler, half a bottle of Spanish plonk, an éclair, and coffee.' He kissed her goodbye. He followed the nurse down the ward until she stopped at the sister's desk.

'Your wife's doing well now,' she said.

'Was it a very bad attack?'

'It was certainly quite a sharp one and she should have come into hospital earlier on, but luckily we managed to get things under control. Of course, the best medicine of all was hearing that the hostages had been released unharmed.'

He thanked her and left.

.   .   .   .   .

Rook stood just inside the strong-room and watched the detective sergeant and detective constable as they worked amongst the chaotic mess and searched for fingerprints. It was a hopeless task. Since the gunmen had all worn gloves and so much was imprinted by people legitimately entitled to have been in there, it was going to be a nightmare of identification and elimination by comparison. But however hopeless, it had to be carried out to try to identify, by some miracle, the fifth bank robber.

He stared at the tens of thousands of notes which littered the floor – the two other detectives were of necessity walking on them as if they were worthless scraps of paper – and then at the valuables which stretched out from the gap in the shelving, like an overflowing cornucopia. God knows how long it was going to take to discover how much was missing. He smiled sourly. How many of the customers' valuables were hot, in the sense that the owners would not want their possessions to be seen by the police or tax officials? His years in the force had taught him that dishonesty wasn't the prerogative of criminals.

He continued to watch the other two for a while, then said: 'How much longer do you reckon to be?'

The detective sergeant, a mournful man from H.Q., stood upright and eased his back. 'A couple of weeks, if we're dead lucky.'

'Then you're going to be dead unlucky. I want the bank staff down here this afternoon.'

'Quite impossible, sir.'

'Then I'll make it late afternoon. The impossible always takes a little longer.'

The detective sergeant looked a shade sourer.

6

Originally, Tudor Cottage had been built for the younger son of a yeoman farmer and therefore it was fairly small. But Penelope had the ability, without spending much money, of filling any house with charm and character and the inside of Tudor Cottage was now more attractive than many larger and architecturally more interesting houses.

Steen sat in the north-east facing sitting-room and stared at the painting he had done two years ago of Penelope. It was the painting of which he was most proud, yet many who saw it didn't like it because they thought it didn't really look like her. He'd finished it soon after she'd been rather ill and in her face was expressed both her capacity for love and her courage. It was strange, he thought wistfully, how he had been able to paint in her character when usually his work was pure 'chocolate-box'.

He didn't understand and/or believe a tithe of the arcane mumbo-jumbo that art experts wrote or said, but he did know that all the truly great paintings offered him something more than their immediate image. He could usually paint only the immediate image because he lacked the force of creation: and if her portrait was a creative work, he'd no idea why it had been an exception.

The phone rang. He left the room, ducking under the lintel of the door, and went into the hall which stretched up in a triangular shape because the space had once been the outshot. The telephone was on a corner cupboard, by the kitchen door.

'Mr Steen? It's Sergeant Raleigh of the county constabulary here. Detective Inspector Rook would be grateful if you could go back to the bank and help sort things out. There's rather a mess in the strong-room.'

'Right away? I haven't cleaned up or had anything to eat yet. My wife's in hospital and I've only just got back.'

'I'm very sorry to hear that . . . Then could you go along as soon as you're ready? We don't like pressing you, but it is rather urgent.'

'I'll get there as soon as I can.'

'That's great.'

After replacing the receiver he went through to the kitchen. In the refrigerator were a portion of veal-and-ham pie, two different sliced meats, liver pâté, bacon, eggs, and a curry left-over. He chose the pie, fried himself some chips, and ate in the kitchen.

He ran the bath – the bathroom was downstairs – and went up to the larger bedroom for fresh clothes. Penelope's woolly Yorkshire Terrier – inside which she kept her nightdress – was not on the double bed. In some way, for him its absence was the most poignant thing about the empty house.

The drive back into Scranton Cross, a distance of four miles through country lanes, took just over twenty minutes because there was a traffic snarl-up at the bridge, under repair, over the river Scrant – for thirty years little more than a stream of pollution. He parked in the usual car-park, finding a space close by where his car had been earlier.

A P.C., who stared blankly at the crowds of curious people who looked in, stood in the porch of the bank. When Steen made to enter, he focussed his gaze and said: 'Bank's closed until further notice.'

'I work here and was phoned to come back in.'

'That's different. Can I have your name, please?' The P.C. took a sheet of paper from his right-hand pocket.

'Steen.'

The P.C. checked with the list. 'That's all right then, sir. Go ahead.' He stepped to one side.

Steen was astonished to find how normal the bank looked: only the presence of two uniform policemen and another man in civvies suggested anything unusual had ever happened. Gaitshead invariably met trouble with the comment, 'Forget it. In two days' time no one will remember what the problem was.' For once, thought Steen, Gaitshead had a point.

Wraight came out of his office, along the open passage, and into the general area. When he saw Steen he said: 'There you are, Bill. Glad you've finally been able to make it.' He looked a pompous, pernickety man and quite often behaved as such, yet always about him was the air of quiet authority.

Steen explained. 'I had to go to the general hospital to see my wife before I grabbed a wash and some food. That's why I've been held up.'

'Your wife is ill and in hospital? I'm very sorry to hear that. Nothing very serious, I trust?'

'A rather sharp attack of asthma.'

'That can be nasty. My wife's sister has it all too regularly. Well, I do hope she's soon very much better.'

'Thanks.'

Wraight coughed, to show they must now get down to business. 'The police want you to help down in the strong-room since you're in charge – nominally – of customers' valuables.' His voice became outraged. 'There's a terrible mess down there. Just sheer vandalism. They've thrown the money about and opened God knows how many cases and distributed their contents all over the place. You'll have to sort out things as best you can and then find somewhere to put everything that's left over so that the customers can come and try to identify their own possessions. Heavens only knows how long it's all going to take. Head office is going to be very, very upset.' Wraight lowered his voice. 'Don't let that rather tiresome detective inspector worry you. We have a way of doing things in this bank and we're not going to alter just for him.'

Although Wraight's agitated words should have warned him, Steen was quite unprepared for the degree of confusion he saw when he went down the stairs into the basement. As he stared into the strong-room, a man stepped out over the very thick, arced sill. Steen saw a humourless face, very heavily lined considering Rook's age, with a sharp mouth and a determined chin. A nasty character to cross, he thought – an opinion he later had cause to remember. 'I'm Bill Steen and I got a phone call . . .'

'I've been waiting a long time for you to turn up.'

'My wife's ill and in hospital and I had to visit he
before going home and changing and eating.' Steen spok
pugnaciously.

'I'm sorry she's ill,' said Rook, but with obvious for
mality. Unfortunately, he took his work too seriously
waste time over minor social conventions. He half turne
and indicated the interior of the strong-room. 'You ca
see what things are like – a goddamn mess. Two of you
blokes are sorting out the money and counting it to dis
cover how much has gone: I want you to get cracking o
the valuables.'

'How can any money be gone? You caught the gun
men.'

'One of 'em managed to escape,' muttered Rook, hi
tone momentarily defensive. 'I'm assuming he took a
much money with him as he could. He may also hav
taken a handful of jewellery – a load of diamond
wrenched out of their settings, although they'd be mor
dangerous to him when it came to unloading them. I wa
you to find out.'

'That's not going to be easy.'

'I know. I had a lecture from your manager. He say
when you take in a container from the customer yo
carefully don't ask what's inside. All you write down a
date, name, and description of container.'

'That's the way they want it.'

'Seeing what some of the cases contained, I'm n
surprised. . . . How long d'you suppose it'll take you
identify everything and find out what's missing?'

How long was a piece of string? 'First off, I'll have
sort things out as far as I can. Then I'll have to wa
until customers have come and identified what's their
It'll take days, at the very least. Might be weeks if som
people don't bother to turn up quickly. It could even b

that some are dead and never told anyone they'd got stuff stored here. We've cases that have been in for years.'

Rook swore, although it was the answer he had been expecting.

'What could speed things up is to get the press and TV to say customers ought to come along to the bank to check.'

'I've laid that on already.'

Steen waited, but when the detective inspector continued to stare moodily down at the floor he went round him and into the strong-room. Seebring and Hodges were working at the table, sorting out the bank notes. As Steen entered, Seebring dropped a load of notes on to the table. 'They've dragged you back as well, have they?' His tone became petulant. 'The rest of the staff can stay at home and recover, but we poor bastards get dragged back willy-nilly, regardless of how we feel.'

Hodges said: 'You should feel honoured at being chosen.' He had a mocking, ironic manner.

'Maybe we'll get a medal.' Steen looked at the gap between the shelving and at the valuables which had spilled out through it. He saw an elaborate tiara which, as he moved his head slightly, sparkled with icy blue pinpoints of colour. If that were genuine – and there was every reason to suppose it was – it would be worth a fortune. Near it was a diamond necklace which looked to be of the same design in the setting.

Seebring noticed where he was looking. 'Some of the family jewels – of the less intimate kind! Who d'you reckon they belong to? Old Mrs Marchton?'

'If so, that's the biggest waste of assets we'll ever come across,' said Hodges, as he slipped a rubber band over a wad of two hundred five-pound notes and then tossed

49

them on to a small pile of bundles of similar denomination on the floor.

Steen walked over and looked closely at the tiara and necklace. The intricate settings were beautifully made and chased and he found them far more attractive than the diamonds. It was sad to think that perhaps they did belong to Mrs Marchton, widow of a millionaire, who always looked as if she needed a bath and change of clothes. How long since the jewellery had been worn? Did anyone but royalty wear tiaras these days? In terms of capital they would have been appreciating over the years, but what a useless, totally barren appreciation. Tens of thousands of pounds which were so buried away that not even the beauty was available to give pleasure. He looked beyond the ends of the shelves and saw, on top of a pile of objects, a wooden box, the lid of which had been wrenched open, in which was a porcelain kingfisher, brilliantly coloured, stretched in curving, darting flight. A Dorothy Doughty? More beauty, more capital, locked away. How much were all the valuables here worth? A million? A million pounds, owned by people who were so rich that they could afford to let it lie in the dark.

'Blimey, Bill, what's up with you?' asked Seebring. 'You look like . . . like . . .' He couldn't find a satisfactory simile.

'Just feeling a bit worn-out,' replied Steen, reluctant to give any hint of what he'd been thinking.

'Me also. It's not surprising, is it? They'd no right to drag us back here instead of leaving us at home, like the rest of 'em. Look, if you don't feel up to working, you go and tell the old man you're off and if he doesn't like it he can take a running jump.' Seebring was always encouraging other members of the staff to revolt, but never himself led the way.

'It's probably because it's hot in here. I'll get used to it.'

'If I'd've known I was going to end up hour after hour in this heat, I'd've had a word with the union bloke. There ought to be air conditioning down here.'

Rook stepped over the sill into the strong-room. 'How's it going, then?' he asked, in a critical voice.

'Tell him,' suggested Hodges.

Seebring resumed work. 'It's a long, long job,' he observed.

Rook spoke to Steen. 'Are you going to start sorting things out, then?'

'Sure. I didn't hear the whistle blow, though.'

Rook belatedly realized the need for a more diplomatic approach. 'I'm sorry we've had to bring you back here like this, but it's absolutely vital for us to find out what's missing. If it's money, you'll be able to give us some numbers of notes, if it's jewellery, we should be able to get descriptions. Get them circulated and we've a much better chance of nabbing the missing villain.'

Steen nodded and carefully climbed over the confusion of cases and valuables to get into the far space. He looked around. The shelves had originally been about three-quarters filled and the best estimate he could now make was that a good half of all the containers had been opened and their contents dumped.

To sort out the mess surely qualified as the thirteenth labour of Hercules. He'd need a table, the deposit and withdrawal book, the patience of Job . . .

There was a foot high heap of valuables close to where he stood and he saw rings, necklaces, silver candelabra, tureens, gold coins, and stamp albums. He picked up one of the coins which glowed warmly in the overhead light. For a coin, it was heavy. It was French, a Louis, and dated from the reign of Louis the Thirteenth. So how much was that worth? He saw another gold coin and picked it up, to find it was a double pistole, a doubloon. A pirate's treasure. In his mind he saw square-rigged ships in mortal battle . . .

After his first few days in the bank, money had become a mere symbol without any meaning or real value. A thousand was not a new car (as it had once been), but was so many notes at such and such denominations. But suddenly he was once again identifying wealth as wealth: the gold coins, the diamond tiara and necklace, the porcelain kingfisher, represented a small fortune. Why should a few people have so much money they didn't need it all, while so many had much less than they honestly needed? The tiara alone would take Penelope to the sun . . . Hell! he suddenly thought, if Wraight could read his thoughts at that moment he'd be sacked.

He began the job of sorting through the chaos.

7

Steen, grunting from the effort, moved the tea-chest along the shelves. He straightened up and mopped his face and neck with a handkerchief. That was the last of the undamaged containers and it was now clear that not quite as many had been ripped open as at first had seemed possible. Thank God for small mercies! Now to sort out the owners and list their names and, by elimination, find out which customers had had their possessions tampered with.

He went to the small wooden box built in at one end of the shelves, opened this, and took out the deposit and withdrawal book, dirty and dating back a great number of years. A description of the container was entered by the depositing clerk, along with the date and the customer's name, and the customer signed the entry. The container was then brought down to the strong-room and if labelled and locked, lashed down beyond immediate tampering, or sealed, (preferably all four), was stored: if it wasn't sufficiently well-secured, the depositing clerk used label, twine, sealing-wax and a bank seal, all kept in the wooden box, to rectify the fault before putting the container on the shelves.

Steen examined the nearest suitcase, medium-sized, metal-cornered, brown and shabby, and swore when he could find no name: obviously there had been a sticky label which had come off. He opened the deposit and withdrawal book and skimmed through the entries for the last year and found no medium-sized, metal-cornered, brown suitcase. He swore again. This was supposed to be the easy part of the job! He went back two years and almost immediately found the entry. He put a mark by the name in the book and wrote the name down at the top of a sheet of foolscap paper, then made out a label and stuck it on.

The next container was a cardboard shoe box which had been festooned with string, with each knot sealed with an unimpressed grey-flecked green sealing-wax. The name Smithson was written in ink. The name was familiar and as he noted it he tried to put a face to it.

He went to check a third case, but then stopped because something was worrying him. At first he couldn't identify that something, but soon recognized that it was one of the entries which he'd fleetingly noticed in his search through the deposit and withdrawal book. He returned to where he'd left the book and opened it at the last page of entries. The final one was in a handwriting he did not recognize. He thought back. On Tuesday – the last normal working day at the bank – he had been called to accept a deposit not long before the bank closed: the deposit had been a small cardboard box which he had had to seal. By the time he'd finished dealing with it, there'd been only minutes left. He'd gone up top and back along to his open-plan office, just beyond the 'Foreign Business' counter. No one had passed him going down to the strong-room with an article to deposit and he was quite certain that no customer had deposited anything once he'd been in his office. He examined the final entry more closely. In form, it was correct. Date, the fifteenth: name, A. R. Parsons: description, one large brown expanding suitcase, roped and sealed. But the writing was quite unknown to him. Nominally he was in charge of deposits and withdrawals, but in practice he was so often busy that another member of the staff dealt with the matter. Even so, the person concerned was usually one of four people. Had everything been so busy Tuesday afternoon, just before three o'clock, that a member of the staff who had never before dealt with valuables had had to deal with this suitcase? Yet Tuesday had for once – it was market day – been a slack afternoon.

Curiosity made him search along the shelves for a brown, expanding, roped and sealed suitcase with the name of A. R. Parsons. He soon found it. It was bound with bank twine, sealed with the colour of sealing-wax which the bank was currently using and the seals were impressed with the bank's seal. On the face of things, absolutely in order. He looked at the label, then back at the book as he tried to think who could have handled this and how the deposit had been made without his knowledge and he suddenly noticed – his interest having been so alerted – that there was a distinct similarity in form not only between the capital R in the book entry and on the label, which was perfectly feasible, but also between those two Rs and the Rs of the signatures, which was not feasible since the first must have been written by a bank employee while the signatures were the customer's.

He had the kind of sharp, vivid imagination which could be both visionary and practical and he now stared at the suitcase and let his mind run riot. The police and Wraight had assumed that the strong-room had been left in a shambles as an act of bloody-minded vandalism. But suppose the real reason was to make certain that for several hours no one could check whether anything were missing? A lot of money, in the higher denomination notes, could be stuffed into a large suitcase. That suitcase could be renamed, lashed up and sealed with the bank seal (kept in the wooden box). When someone came to withdraw the suitcase (one gunman had escaped – because he had to organize the withdrawal, not for the far more obvious reason that he wished to be free?) and the police asked him if it was in order, he'd point to the unbroken seals. He'd be able to walk out of the bank without a moment's suspicion touching him. . . .

He stared at the suitcase.

·   ·   ·   ·   ·

Dutch Keen was as English as roast beef and Yorkshire pudding, but he had once sailed as a cabin boy on a Dutch cargo ship. He was an intelligent man, with a quick brain and a natural histrionic gift. His face was slightly pear-shaped and he used his facial muscles more than most so that he was a man of many expressions. Had he not been an alcoholic he could have been either a good actor or a really successful con-man.

Drude stood in the centre of the poorly furnished room and stared at Keen. 'You've got to play it real smooth.'

'No problem, no problem at all,' replied Keen, in a rounded, self-satisfied, slightly condescending voice.

'And keep off the booze.'

'When I undertake a job . . .'

'You spread this and you'll never spread another job.'

'Please, stop fussing. I assure you, the matter is as good as done.' For him at that point, failure was inconceivable.

'Are you sure you can do the signature good enough?'

'I've practised it until Mr Parsons himself would be unable to tell the difference.' Keen suddenly sniggered and there was something disquieting in the contrast between that snigger and his previous portentous speech.

'Then get moving.'

Keen crossed the threadbare carpet and stood in front of the tarnished gilt mirror. He slightly adjusted the set of his tie, then studied his general reflection. He smiled with quiet satisfaction. Every inch the retired army officer.

.   .   .   .   .

As Steen continued to work, his thoughts mostly stayed with that brown suitcase. If it were filled with notes of the higher denominations – probably not too many twenties because they were traceable since their numbers were kept – how much would it contain? Not quite certain why, or perhaps not yet admitting why, he looked over the cases and through the shelves to see if Seebring and

Hodges were at all interested in what he was doing. They weren't.

A large sum of money would buy unlimited sunshine and unpolluted air . . . He tried to slam a door on his thoughts. But, suddenly, wealth had come to have too much real meaning to allow him to slam the door shut.

To steal from the bank would be to damn his soul, never mind the danger, because he was old-fashioned enough to believe in an honourable soul. If placed in a position of responsibility, one honoured that responsibility through hell and high water. . . . But here possibly the money had already virtually been stolen: but for his having made the penultimate entry in the book so late on Tuesday afternoon, he – and certainly no one else – would not have the slightest idea of what had, possibly, happened. . . . To steal money already stolen was surely not breaking the honour he owed the bank? In any case, in the final event honour could never be more important than health. And did a starving man commit theft when he took a piece of bread from a baker who'd baked so much that a lot of loaves were being left to go stale?

He reached out and touched the twine bindings of the suitcase. No one could ever know whether they had been cut during or after the siege: the whole area was littered with slashed twine. So he could safely cut the bindings and open the case (if it were locked, there was a huge bunch of keys amassed from God knows where, one of which would almost certainly unlock it). And if it was not filled with bank notes he'd be quite safe, except perhaps from his conscience. On the other hand, if it were filled with notes . . .

He looked between the shelves at Seebring and Hodges once more. They were taking no more notice of him now – they could not see what he was doing from where they sat – than before. He put his hand in his coat pocket and withdrew a penknife.

He cut the twine with frantic haste, dragged it free and threw it down on the floor, alongside other cut twine. He discovered he was breathing heavily and sweating freely.

He heard Seebring speak. 'My fingers are aching like they were broken. What's more, I'm getting spots before my eyes. Someone bloody well ought to get hold of Wraight and tell him he's got to find reliefs for us.'

'So what's stopping you?' asked Hodges.

Seebring ignored the inconvenient question. 'It's just not fair to saddle us with all the work. How long have we been down here now . . . ?'

Steen tried the right-hand lock, expecting it to be fastened, and it snapped up with a sound that seemed deafening. Terrified, he looked through the shelves to discover the two men at the table were still taking no notice of him. He opened the left-hand lock, careful initially to hold down the flap, and released it slowly so that it made no noise. He raised the lid of the case. As he stared down at the bundles of notes in their original brown-paper wrappings, wedged in place by loose notes, he knew a sick excitement.

Penelope's health lay in that suitcase. Because of the two opposed sides of his imagination he could see at least some of the problems that would occur if he took this money. When the police learned how large a sum of money was missing they'd very soon work out what had happened. He'd be asked why he hadn't noticed that last entry and identified it as false. . . . How to work the switch? . . . How to get the money out of the bank? . . . If ever the police began to suspect one of the staff had switched the money, they'd surely look for signs of sudden wealth. . . . How could he spend money taking Penelope to live abroad and yet hide the origin of the money? . . .

Someone must soon come for the suitcase because it had to be claimed before the money remaining was totalled and the true extent of the loss discovered. If he were to make the switch he needed another container which almost certainly would not be claimed. . . . There were several containers which had been in store for years, probably because their owners were dead and none of the beneficiaries had known of the deposit (such containers were known as coffins).

The deposit and withdrawal book identified a coffin which had been in store for over ten years. He found the suitcase, dusty, locked but not roped. He lifted it up and judged it to be near enough the same weight – somewhere around eighty pounds. He collected the large bunch of keys and tried each in turn and finally unlocked the case to discover it was filled with papers and files. He transferred the money to the dusty green case and the papers to the expanding brown suitcase.

The green suitcase was labelled – with an engraved visiting card – Geoffrey Braynton. He removed this and replaced it with one of the bank's labels. He chose the name, which he wrote in block capitals, T. Edey. It was only later that he realized this was the name of a schoolmaster he had disliked. He dirtied the label and retied the rope, then replaced the suitcase with those he had checked. He lashed the brown suitcase with twine in the same pattern as before. He used a stick of sealing-wax and his lighter to drop sealing-wax on to the knots, which he stamped with the bank seal.

'Are you brewing up tea?' called out Seebring facetiously, 'because if you are I could go a cuppa?'

He knew momentary panic, shocked that he could so easily have overlooked the smell of melting wax. Then he

59

forced himself to calm and said: 'Just replacing a seal that's broken off.'

It was so normal a thing for him to be doing that Seebring was immediately uninterested. 'You'd've thought, wouldn't you, that the old man would've at least laid on something for us to eat and drink? Not him, though. I've a good mind to . . .'

Steen replaced the sealing-wax, the twine, and seal, in the wooden box. Then he opened the deposit and withdrawal book and drew a line through the entry of G. Braynton to show the case had been withdrawn: he added a scrambled signature and a date of four years back.

He stared at the two suitcases, now side-by-side. It never occurred to him to wonder what the mob's reactions would be.

8

Dutch Keen, playing the retired colonel so thoroughly that his stride was firm and measured, his shoulders squared, and there was a look of sharp authority on his face, marched along the pavement until he reached an electrical store. He stopped, turned smartly to his right, and appeared to look at the window display. In the reflection of the glass he was able to judge that there was no particular police activity around the bank.

He crossed the road and reached the far pavement immediately opposite the main bank entrance. There was still a P.C. in the porch entrance and as he approached, the P.C. said: 'I'm afraid the bank's shut. . . .'

'I heard there'd been trouble,' he said crisply. 'Matter of fact, I've come to see about some stuff I left here. Be a bit of a blow if I've lost it. D'you know how I can find out?'

'You've deposited something in the strong-room, sir?'

'A suitcase. Got a few mementoes in it I've picked up from different places.'

'If you'll go inside, then, sir. The detective sergeant is checking up on the valuables and he'll have a word with you.'

'Thanks very much.' He walked past the P.C. and into the bank.

Inside, he looked around with the confident air of a man who had never known what it was like to have his over-draft bouncing its limit. Young saw him, and even he, a natural iconoclast, made a quick mental note that here was someone of some importance. He went over.

Keen explained in his chatty yet authoritative manner that he had only recently deposited a suitcase with the bank for safe keeping, but he'd heard there'd been some kind of robbery and wanted to make certain his mementoes were all right.'

'What's the name, please?' asked Young.

'Parsons. Colonel A. R. Parsons. Though these days I forget the colonel part.'

So I should bloody well think, thought Young as he turned and left.

    .   .   .   .   .

Steen was placing two pearl rings with other jewellery found loose when Young stepped into the strong-room and stopped by the gap in the shelves. 'Have you come across a suitcase belonging to an old colonel sahib from Poona, name of Parsons?'

Steen turned to conceal his sudden panicky tension. 'I'll check,' he said, hoping his voice hadn't sounded too croaky. He picked up the list of undamaged containers and appeared to study it. This was the last moment at which he could withdraw. If he said he couldn't find the case, 'Parsons' would be asked to go away and return the next day. In the meantime, he could either 'discover' what had happened or switch the money back and await events. . . . He put the paper down, turned, walked back along the shelves and searched until he found the brown suitcase. He picked it off the shelf.

'Will you take it up?' asked Young.

'Depends whether you want this job down here done in a hurry?'

Young swore. Steen said: 'Get him to sign for it if he's taking it away, will you?' He handed over the book, opened at the last page of entries. 'In that last column.'

Young took the book in his left hand and picked up the suitcase with his right. 'What the hell's he got in here?' He readjusted his balance. 'A bloody elephant shot on the banks of the Limpopo?' He left.

.   .   .   .

Keen parked the car and walked along to his digs – his walk was now far less purposeful and he no longer held himself so erect. He reached the brown-fronted house, climbed the three stone steps, and unlocked the front door. Inside, he went up to his room which was at the end of the passage on the first floor.

Drude, who'd been pacing the floor and was up by the window, swung round.

'There we are,' said Keen, with loud satisfaction as he put the suitcase down on the floor. 'Just like picking cherries off a tree.'

'The police . . .'

'Couldn't have been more helpful. Brought the case up to me, asked me to sign for it, and that was the beginning and end of everything.' He crossed to the built-in clothes cupboard, opened the right-hand door, reached down and brought out a bottle of whisky. 'We'll have a drink on it.' He put the bottle down on the table, went back to the cupboard for glasses. He poured out two drinks and handed one glass to Drude.

'Let's have some water,' said Drude curtly.

'You'll have to use the tap.'

Drude, his expression contemptuous, went over to the cracked wash-hand-basin.

Keen drank eagerly and emptied the glass. He looked at Drude, then poured himself out a second and larger drink. 'Well – are you going to open up?' He tapped the suitcase with the toe of his shoe.

'No.'

'Why not? Surely you want to see . . .'

'You've finished your job. Now forget it.'

'All right. If that's the way you feel . . .'

'That's the way.' Drude finished his whisky and put the glass down. He laid the suitcase flat to check the seals.

'How about my grand?' said Keen.

Satisfied the seals were intact, Drude took a bundle of notes from his pocket and threw it on to the unmade bed. 'Open your mouth once on this, Dutch, and you'll be feeding the rats.'

'As if I'd be so bloody silly.' He looked at the bottle, then at Drude's glass on the table. 'Would you like another drink. . . ?'

'I wouldn't. And nor would you.' Drude picked up the suitcase, not without a grunt of surprise at its weight, and left. He went down the stairs, out on to the pavement, and turned to go along to where he'd parked. How much was in the suitcase? Val had never given a figure, but it weighed enough for a million. If only he dared open it . . . But that would be to sign his own death warrant. That suitcase wasn't going to be opened until everyone was there to see the seals were unbroken. Only in that way could they all be certain none of the others was twisting them.

. . . . . .

At six-thirty Steen came through into the first half of the strong-room. Seebring, his eyes red, said: 'Going to have a breather, then?'

'I'm packing it in for the night.'

'You're what?' Seebring was uneasily surprised. 'But the old man said we'd got to get the job done as quickly as possible.'

'He's going to be unlucky, isn't he?'

Seebring was envious of Steen's declared independence, at the same time as he was vaguely hopeful that such independence would lead to trouble.

Steen left after saying good night. Up top Young, standing near the outer doors, was talking to another man in civvies. When he saw Steen approach he cut short what he'd been saying and spoke to Steen. 'Is it all finished, then?'

'There's a hell of a long way to go yet. But my wife's in hospital and I'm going to visit her.'

'Yeah, of course. Have you any idea how much longer you'll be?'

'It'll take the whole of tomorrow morning at least just to sort out and list everything that's loose.'

'I told the old man it would be a lot longer job than he reckoned.'

Steen nodded good night and went out. He crossed the road to the long island which separated the through one-way traffic from the loading and unloading traffic, waited for a break in the stream of cars, then continued over to the narrow passage which ran down the side of the cinema to the council car-park.

To the north of Scranton Cross there were still a number of large Victorian and Edwardian houses, sturdy if not elegant, set in large gardens and clearly the homes of wealthy people. In the past, when he'd had occasion to drive past these houses, he'd thought how wonderful it must be to live in one of them since then money could not be one of the main problems in life. Now, he was potentially rich enough that money would no longer be a problem in his . . . except the problem of how to go about spending it. No matter what happened, he must move very slowly and exactly as he had planned.

The hospital was set in well tended grounds and he parked in front of a bed of roses, to remember that in his hurry he'd forgotten to bring any flowers for Penelope. He climbed out of the car, stared at a brilliant yellow bloom and wondered if he dared pick that and take it to her. There were few people in sight and all were busy about their own business. He leaned over and snapped off the stem with the bloom. When he straightened up he checked again, to discover he'd been unobserved. Only then did it strike him how ridiculous it was that he should be worried over being caught scrumping a single rose bloom when he was in the middle of stealing a fortune.

Penelope had some colour back in her cheeks. He kissed her and for a brief moment — brief because she disliked any public display of sentiment — she put her right arm round him and hugged him. When she released him, he sat on the edge of the bed. 'How are things now, darling?'

'I'm a hundred times better, thanks to knowing that you are all right.' She had been studying his face and now she frowned. 'But you look . . . Bill, are *you* all right?'

'Of course I am.'

'You look very tired. . . . And something else.'

'It's all just tiredness. I've been back at the bank, clearing up some of the mess and trying to sort out what's missing.'

'Are you sure it's not delayed shock?'

He laughed. 'Nothing so interesting! By the way, I've brought you this.' He handed her the yellow rosebud.

She gave a quick exclamation of delight. 'But how lovely! Where on earth's it from? We've no rose like this in the garden.'

'You force me to confess. I've just pinched it from near where I parked.'

'Bill, you really are the limit sometimes! But it i lovely and I don't suppose they'll miss just one . . . I've some wonderful news. If I carry on as I am, I'll be ou on Monday.'

'Terrific. Then you really are getting better?'

'Didn't I tell you I was?'

'You did, but when it comes to your health you can b an awful liar!'

She briefly rested her hand on his. 'I hate being ill s

often: it makes me feel a useless wife and certain you wish you'd married somebody nice and healthy.'

'Shut up,' he said softly. After a pause, he asked her: 'Everything ought to be more organized tomorrow, so is there anything you'd like me to bring? How about some fruit?'

'Not unless you can find some really firm apples. But don't get them if they're too expensive — fruit can be a ridiculous price at this time of the year.'

'If I see any I'll get them before asking what they cost.'

'Hang the expenses,' she said, with loving mockery.

'Talking about expenses, that reminds me — do you remember my talking about Uncle Silas?'

She thought back. 'Wasn't he your father's brother who had a row with the family and left home, never to be heard of again?'

'He got friendly with the family maid and when it became all too obvious that she wasn't a maid any longer my grandfather, who apparently was the epitome of the stern Victorian, kicked him out of house and home. He vanished and even when his parents died no one heard a word from him. Father always said he must be dead. Well, he wasn't and isn't. I've just had a letter from him.'

'Good heavens!'

'It was pretty short, considering all that's happened, and very matter-of-fact, as if uncles often disappear for several dozen years. He said he'd finally settled down after wandering around the world because his health isn't very good now. He'd read that both my parents had died and asked me to tell him how I was, together with news on one or two other people who I don't know anything about.'

'You must ask him along. The poor old boy is probably

as lonely as hell and wants to talk to someone from the family, even if he never knew you.'

'I'd get on to him right away if he lived in England, but he's settled in Mallorca. And come to that, how do we know he's lonely? He may have a wife and ten children along with him.'

'Then he'd have mentioned them in his letter.'

'I suppose you're right. Anyone with ten children would surely not easily overlook them.'

'Have you written back?'

'Give me a chance. I only picked up the letter when I went back home after seeing you this morning.'

'Don't leave it for long – I'll bet he's waiting and waiting for an answer . . . Bill, if I do come back on Monday morning, I'm going to get you that special meal.'

'I'll be doing the cooking until . . .'

'No, you won't,' she said.

He knew that no matter how weak she felt on Monday when she returned home she would cook because her will-power was so much stronger than her body. He thought of the money in the suitcase and knew he'd have done the same thing a dozen times over in order to buy her the health to match her spirit.

9

Drude drove up the M1 to the Northampton junction and then cut across country to Meddlesham, reaching the outskirts of the town as dusk was melting into night. He lost himself once in the maze of back streets, but a man selling evening newspapers directed him to McIntosh Road, where he parked a little down from number four.

Venables opened the front door. He was not as tall as Drude, or as broadly shouldered, yet there was something about the expression of his heavily lined, long face which made Drude immediately wary, almost apprehensive — a most unusual attitude for him.

'Val told me to make contact,' said Drude.

'Do I know Val?' Venables had a voice which was even in tone and almost devoid of inflexion.

'Val Thomas.'

Venables opened the door fully.

They went into the sitting-room in which a woman with tight curly blonde hair, wearing a dress with a neckline that plunged down out of its depth, was watching a large colour television set. She looked round at Drude with interest, then grimaced petulantly when Venables told her to clear out. She walked with swinging hips across the room and slammed the door shut after herself.

'Well?' asked Venables, as he sat.

Drude cleared his throat. 'I was in the bank job with Val.' He expected Venables to show some surprise — even admiration — but Venables seemed indifferent to the news. 'He and me fixed it for me to scramble out as one of the hostages so as I could contact you. He wants a job done and says there's no one near your class for doing it.'

Venables said: 'What's the job?'

'Springing him and Ginger, Alf, and Flash, before the trial.'

Venables took a cigar, in a metal container, from his pocket. He undid the lid, slid out the cigar, and cut the end with finickity care. He struck a match and waited until the head had ceased flaring, then lit the cigar. He drew on the cigar and savoured the rich smoke. 'So why come to me?'

'Val said you was the only one able to do it for sure.'

'I'm flattered.' He sounded bored.

'Are you on?'

Venables rolled the cigar between thumb and forefinger and the smoke rose in lazy curves. 'No.'

Drude could not contain his astonishment. 'But he said you'd do it.'

'Then you'd best see him and tell him he was wrong.'

'He's offering five grand.'

'Where would he get that sort of money, seein' the splits would've skint him when they took him out of the bank?'

Drude regained some of his self-confidence. Venables might act like he was bored, but he couldn't close his ears to the sound of money. 'I've got it, in folding.'

'Five grand for springing four blokes? Great sense of humour, has Val.'

The bargaining went on a long time and eventually Drude settled at seventeen thousand pounds for the job, expenses included, five thousand payable immediately.

. . . .

Rook sat in the chair behind the manager's desk and stared at the far wall. His eyelids dropped and his eyes ached as they struggled for the release of sleep. The picture on the wall, a reproduction of a Constable, grew a second and fuzzy image. His eyes shut and he enjoyed the peace of sleep for seconds, before his head jerked forward to wake him up. It was like being drunk without having had the pleasure of drinking, he thought bitterly.

The door opened and Young, looking irritatingly fresh,

entered. 'They've finished counting the money and they've double-checked the totals.'

Rook had to concentrate to make sense of the words. 'Well?' he finally asked. 'How much did that fly bastard take off with?'

Young didn't answer directly, but pulled a chair to himself and sat down. 'Are you ready for the shock of the century?'

'Let's have the facts without the commentary.'

Young smiled maliciously. 'Three hundred thousand, half of it in tens.'

Rook, suddenly fully awake, stared at him. 'That's got to be nonsense. We're certain the villain who escaped wouldn't have taken twenties, so the outside limit he could have had on him was around thirty thousand. We had that re-run of the TV tape and none of the males was carrying any sort of a bag. . . . The bank clerks have made a balls-up.'

'I told you, they ran a double check because I ordered it. Damn near had a mutiny on account of it. There's three hundred thousand quid missing: fifty thou in twenties, a hundred and fifty thou in tens, and a hundred thou in fivers.'

An old detective sergeant had once told Rook something which had stuck in his mind ever since because a basic fact of detection was buried under the glaring obviousness. 'If a thing's impossible, it can't happen: if it's happened, it wasn't impossible.'

He lit a cigarette. Could the escaped villain have somehow taken three hundred thousand with him? Money in quantity weighed surprisingly heavily and in any case that number of notes – in the tens of thousands – would have been far, far too bulky to hide about the person. . . . But since the police had been in the bank from the end of

71

the siege it was quite impossible. . . . He forced himself, following the detective sergeant's maxim, to turn things round. How had the money been lifted from the bank under the very noses of the police? After a while, his tired brain reached the only possible answer.

He silently swore. Mellon would try to break him for this.

.　　.　　.　　　.　　.　.　　　.

Steen went to bed early and read for only a couple of minutes before the type became fuzzy. He switched off the light and was asleep before he had time to think about the extraordinary events of the day. He was in the middle of a dream, surrealistic in style, when something woke him. After a time he identified that something as a hammering on the front door.

His mind woolly, he switched on the light. He crossed to the south facing, opened window and after moving the curtain aside he leaned out. 'What the hell's up?'

'I was beginning to think I'd have to drop a bomb to wake you. Sorry to bother you, it's Detective Sergeant Young.'

'For God's sake. I was fast asleep . . .'

'I wouldn't be here, Mr Steen, if it weren't very urgent.'

He returned to the bed to pick up his dressing-gown and abruptly his vague resentment gave way to a growing panic because he could only conceive that this middle of the night visit must herald his arrest.

He went down the stairs into the triangular-shaped hall and switched on the light in the porch which enabled him to see the detective sergeant without being clearly seen himself. Young, carrying a plastic bag, was on his own.

Would he have been, had he come to make an arrest? And hadn't his manner been jovial rather than formal? Keep cool, Steen told himself. Take time to think over the answer to every question. He unlocked the front door and Young came through the porch to the hall.

'I'm real sorry about this,' said Young breezily, 'but my D.I.'s acting like he's sitting on a volcano with the crater touching a soft spot. I told him you'd be very fast asleep after what you've been through, but all he said was . . . On second thoughts, I'll forget what he said. Now, if we could just go somewhere and have a sit and a chat, I'll explain what the panic is. By God, it's hot tonight, isn't it?'

'Yes.'

'Good for the breweries, I suppose.'

It was a very crude hint, but nothing else would have registered right then. Steen said: 'Would you like a cold beer?'

'Those words are pure music.'

He opened the sitting-room door and switched on two of the standard lamps, then left Young and went along to the kitchen. He uncapped a couple of bottles of lager, carried glasses and bottles along to the sitting-room.

'First today,' said Young, 'and ten times welcome for it.' He drank eagerly. 'Now I feel more human, I'll tell you what the trouble is.' He opened the plastic bag and brought out of it the deposit and withdrawal book. 'Take a gander at that, will you, and tell me if anything about it strikes you as odd.'

Very conscious that he must appear to do everything naturally – an inhibiting necessity – Steen opened the book and leafed through it. 'What exactly am I supposed to be looking at?'

'Try the end page with entries.'

How soon should he draw attention to that last entry?

'Which of the entries are in your writing?'

He counted them. 'Seven deposits and two withdrawals.'

'Can you say who handled the other three movements?'

'George Abrahams did two of them – not that you'd believe those could be his initials.'

'And the third?'

Steen studied it. 'Frankly, I don't know.'

'Shouldn't you?'

'In theory, yes: in practice I'm often too busy to cope and one of the other staff handles the deposit or withdrawal. This must be someone who hasn't done it before.' He paused, then said: 'When I think about it, that really is odd. I handled the penultimate deposit and it was pretty late on Tuesday afternoon.'

'How late?'

'Within a few minutes of shutting up shop to the public . . . Yet according to this there was another deposit after that one.' He looked up and frowned. 'I didn't see anyone with a suitcase on my way up from the strongroom and certainly no one made a deposit after I returned to my desk.'

'Perhaps you were too busy to notice for certain?'

'I don't think so. For a Tuesday, we were slack. No, I'd have said there definitely wasn't a deposit after the one I handled. And yet . . .' He looked down at the book once more.

'It's a pity you didn't notice that much earlier in the day,' said Young.

.   .   .   .   .   .

The reporters picked up the story on Saturday and it was printed in the Sunday papers.

Thomas, because he was on remand, was allowed to buy whatever papers he wanted and he read the story in the *Sunday Express*. Three hundred thousand altogether, slipped out from under the noses of the splits. It'd make a dying cat laugh. He began to calculate what his share would be, allowing that all Drude had taken with him would go on expenses.

IO

July brought a sharp change of weather: days became cloudy and by the fourth the sky was darkly overcast and the air smelled damp.

Drude walked into the solicitor's office and winked at the receptionist. 'Is his nibs in?' he asked.

'I'll see if Mr Smith is available,' she said. As she pressed down the call switch on the small inter-office telephone exchange, she noted the smart way the coat sat on his broad shoulders: that had never seen the inside of a multiple tailors. She spoke to Smith's personal secretary, then said, 'He's free just for a moment. Do you know the way?'

'Sure.' He winked at her again, opened the door marked 'Private', and went along the short corridor to the office.

Smith was tall and thin and he had a patrician

featured head which was topped by grey hair. His appearance suggested a character so upright as not fully to understand and sympathize with the more outrageous foibles of a few of his clients. Once upon a time, his appearance would not have been a liar.

Drude spoke brashly. 'You've got to get another remand at the next hearing.'

Smith stared out through the window. Regretfully, he still suffered from just enough pride – it was difficult to know why – to be angered by Drude's attitude. But he could not afford prideful anger. He said quietly: 'It's not going to be easy: the police naturally want a quick trial. I'll do my best, but if they . . .'

'Balls to that. You just get a further remand.'

He wondered why they wanted to prolong things when they'd been caught red-handed so that there was no feasible defence open to them and their only real hope must be to try for a lesser sentence than armed robbery and hostage taking usually received?

.   .   .   .   .

The justices of the peace, chaired by a retired county councillor, were far too intent on maintaining the majesty of their position to wonder why the defence solicitor was obviously so passionately eager to gain a further remand. And thus, when the police forcefully argued that the defence had had plenty of time to prepare their case – what case? – the J.P.s allowed the remand order to show everyone that they, and not the police, were in charge of events.

.   .   .   .   .

During the day the strong-room was, of necessity always open and the huge circular door with its locking lugs withdrawn was kept swung right back. Since there was only one way of reaching it, down the stairs in the basement, no one could get to it without being observed by other members of the staff – especially since Miss Tucker worked at the nearest point to the doorway at the end of the open passage.

Steen walked towards the doorway and smiled at Miss Tucker. In return, she gave him a toothy smile in which there was little warmth: wrongly, she bracketed him with Gaitshead.

He went down the stairs. Deeding was inside the strong-room, searching through the drawers of one of the filing cabinets and he looked up. 'Hey, Bill, have you seen the Walters papers? The old man's screaming his head off for 'em. I could've sworn they were here.'

He stepped over the circular sill. 'I haven't seen 'em for weeks.'

'Well, he's not going to get them today, that's for sure.' Deeding looked at his watch.

'Aren't you going to offer to stay on to search every last nook and cranny?'

'That's a dirty joke.' Deeding slammed shut the drawer of the filing cabinet. 'I suppose now I'll have to slide out without him seeing me or I'll get one of his interminable lectures on how things used to be in his day when the staff was keen and loyal.'

'And naught was heard but the scratching of quill pens.'

Deeding grinned. 'Think how peaceful it must have been with no computers to snarl up everything! . . . That's that, then, no Walters papers today.' He walked over to the circular doorway. 'See you tomorrow – provided I don't drop down dead in the meantime.' He left.

77

Steen entered the valuables compartment and looked at his watch again. The tellers would be down in five minutes with their cash floats and other staff would bring the confidential files which had been used during the day. He looked through the shelf area to make certain the strong-room remained empty, even though it must have since he'd have heard anyone who came down the stairs, then he took a key from his coat pocket and unlocked the suitcase marked T. Edey. He stared at the mass of bank notes and felt awe and fear.

He'd made for himself – based on what presumably the escaped bank robber had worn – a cotton money belt with four pockets. He was wearing it and he unbuttoned his shirt, reached down with his right hand, unhooked the belt and withdrew it. He filled one pocket with ten pound and three with five pound notes.

Replacing the money belt when it was filled was, he discovered, far from the easy job practice had suggested it would be. The belt kept ruckling and the pockets collapsed back on each other. In the end he had to undo his trousers, pull up his shirt, and tie the belt around his waist. He had just secured it and was reaching down to pull up his trousers when he heard the clump of heavy footsteps beginning to descend the stairs, followed by the booming voice of Gaitshead.

He suffered a panic which seemed to freeze his limbs. Then he managed to regain some self-control, went to draw up his trousers and realized the open suitcase was far less easily explained and shut that first. He pulled up his trousers, zipped them, buttoned up his shirt and was astonished to discover that he had been able to do all this before the leading man, Gaitshead, had reached the foot of the stairs. There was still time for him to lock the suitcase.

'I'm telling you,' said Gaitshead loudly, as he stepped down on to the basement floor, 'she's the neatest, tastiest bit of crackling this side of paradise. And is her old man loaded!'

'It's never advisable to marry for money,' said Cantor, who was peculiarly adept at saying something trite with the utmost sincerity.

'But don't run away too hard if ever you find it, eh?' Gaitshead stepped over the sill but caught his foot, making him have to hop to keep his balance. He swore.

Steen looked down at his waist and checked it didn't bulge. He called out: 'What you need is a brewer's daughter.'

'So you're down here, are you? Slacking again. Some bloke's make life easy for themselves, that's for sure.'

Steen stepped through the gap. 'Just think of the advantages – free beer for the rest of your life.'

'Sure. But what if it's a brand I don't like? Anyway, the only brewer's daughter I've ever met looked like one of their dray horses.'

'You'll never get everything, so decide on your priorities.'

They heard the sound of other people descending and Gaitshead and Cantor began to put away the files they were carrying. Four women, carrying the black metal boxes in which they kept their cash floats, came down into the strong-room.

Steen and Gaitshead left ahead of the others and as they reached the top of the stairs they met Wraight and the chief cashier who were on their way below to close the strong-room and set the time lock.

'Is everything in order?' asked Wraight briskly.

'All's tickettyboo,' replied Gaitshead.

79

Wraight stared briefly at him with obvious disfavour, then carried on and downstairs.

'No sense of humour,' said Gaitshead, when certain Wraight couldn't hear him.

'Would you have much left if your bank had been robbed of three hundred thousand quid?' asked Cantor, who'd come up behind them.

'I wouldn't give a hoot what was missing just so long as none of my personal cash was involved. Why should the old man get his knickers in a twist over it? It's all insured.'

They separated. Gaitshead went into the men's cloak-room, Cantor threaded his way through the open offices to his own, and Steen turned off into his. He checked that, apart from the voluminous collection of ever-changing Bank of England regulations on currency export, the working surface was clear, leaned over to open the cupboard to the right of the typewriter well to make certain Miss Beard had taken all travellers' cheques and foreign currency down to the strong-room. He straightened up and patted his stomach and wondered whether to have his coat buttoned up or unbuttoned.

Wraight returned from the strong-room. He stood in front of his office, visually checked that everything was in order, then said: 'Good night, ladies and gentlemen.'

'Parade dismissed,' murmured Gaitshead predictably.

The staff hurried to leave and Steen, careful to be caught up in the main crush, passed through the door-ways and out on to the pavement. He said good night to Miss Beard – young, pretty, and efficient – and crossed to the island. It had all, he thought worriedly, been too easy. He'd walked out of the bank with several thousands of pounds and no one had even looked at him with doubt, let alone suspicion. The traffic eased and he continued over to the pavement. . . . It was ridiculous to be worried because it had been so easy – who was to suspect, when the police and the staff believed the money had left the bank over a fortnight ago?

When he arrived at Tudor Cottage, Penelope was working in the garden and she came across the lawn to meet him at the gate. 'Hullo, darling, have you had a good day?'

'It's been no worse than usual.' He smiled as he studied her. Colour had returned to her face and the lines of pain and worry had gone. If only, he thought wistfully, he could take her away now . . . But he had to play things slowly if he were to be able to play them through to the end so that she never learned the truth.

'Bill, why are you looking at me like that?'

'Like what? Lecherous or hungry?'

'No, not for once. It was as if . . . As if you weren't certain of something and that something wasn't very nice.'

'Just to show you how inaccurate a face reader you are, I was wondering what's for supper.'

'Yes? . . . I've made an egg and bacon pie and picked the first of the lettuces for a salad.' She spoke doubtfully. 'It's not a very big lettuce. I don't seem to be able to grow them to any size.'

'Never mind, I'll bet it's twice as sweet as a shop one . . . If you don't mind, I thought I'd go up and paint a bit?'

'Of course I don't mind. As supper's cold, we can have it when you've finished.'

'I shan't be very long, but I have an idea which I want to try out.'

She accompanied him into the house, showed him the lettuce, then said she was going to watch a programme on television. He went upstairs and along to the bedroom which officially was his 'studio'.

He undid his trousers, removed the cotton money belt and took from this the four bundles of notes. He crossed to the bookcase against the far wall, which was cupboard space up to two feet high, and opened the right-hand cupboard. Inside was a jumble of sketch books, paint, rags, and bottles. He hid the bank notes in the corner and carefully arranged sketch books over them. Penelope would never inadvertently find the money there. She was a practical and down-to-earth person, yet she viewed his ability as an artist not only in a highly flattering light but also, curiously, with some awe and in consequence she never came into the studio to tidy it up for fear of moving something which might in some way affect his 'inspiration'.

He shut the cupboard door, then crossed to the easel on which was a fresh canvas. He picked up a stick of charcoal and wondered what to sketch in to further his story of having had an idea? . . . And suddenly he had an idea, only it was to do with a way of ensuring he had an accountable income when they were living in Mallorca.

.   .   .   .

Together with all the other jails in the country, Mimblesham Jail had had its security strengthened over the past few years. There were now additional watch towers ensuring that every section of the surrounding fifteen-foot brick wall was under constant watch, the incurving four-stranded barbed-wire fence on top of the wall had been electrified, the floodlighting went right round, two workshops which had been set against an outside wall had been demolished, and a constant patrol with dogs outside the walls was maintained. Built nearly eighty years before in what had then been a rural setting on the outskirts of the town it was now surrounded by houses and the occupants of these houses were encouraged to report anything suspicious, such as a parked car in which the occupants sat for any length of time.

Venables planned the break with imagination, attention to the smallest detail, and complete disregard of the consequences to others. Timing was vital and here they were lucky because two roads away was the parish church of St Joseph: the church clock struck a carillon every hour. H-hour was fixed for five o'clock in the afternoon and the moment of go was to be marked by the end of the carillon and the first stroke of five. At that time Thomas, Chase, Brent, and Jenkins, would be down in the exercise yard on the north side, along with other men on remand.

The necessary cars were stolen early Friday morning. They chose large, powerful cars, but not Jaguars because these were used so often in jobs that there tended to be a question mark over any Jaguar seen near a point of security danger. Two of the cars were driven to Mimblesham and parked in a side road, two more were parked in Cheddington, the next town south to Mimblesham. This offered them a double change-over, greatly lessening the odds of the police's being able to trail them through eye-witnesses' evidence. Of the remaining cars, two were fitted with unprimed fire bombs and the boot of the third was loaded with TXL, a plastic explosive with many times the power of dynamite yet completely harmless unless armed with a detonator.

The last three cars left just after midday and they drove due south for three hours, after which they cut east across country and arrived at Mimblesham at four-thirty. They stopped in a large open car-park, just behind a new shopping centre, and Venables, who drove the lead Ford, under cover of rearranging the luggage in the boot, inserted a detonator in the TXL explosive and coupled this up to a battery and small radio receiver. Halliwell, who sat in the rear seat of the Ford and kept tight hold of an Alsatian bitch, was uncomfortably aware of the fact that he now sat in front of an armed bomb.

They drove out of the car-park at ten to five, Venables taking the Ford west, the Vauxhall and the Rover going south. The Ford entered Minters Lane at three minutes to five. Venables slowed, braked, and peered at the numbers of the houses as if searching for one particular one until Halliwell's croaky voice said that there were only ninety seconds to go. He changed up, increased speed, and went round the corner into Rowley Avenue to come in sight of the prison.

A security guard, his Alsation dog on a leash by his side, had just entered the road from the far end. Venables braked, to bring the car to a halt against the pavement on the left-hand side. Halliwell opened his off-side door and gave the Alsatian bitch a hard push.

The bitch was on heat and when she saw the dog she ran forward. Venables shouted, drew out from the pavement and began to give chase in the car, swerving over to the right-hand side of the road. He pulled up by the wall as the bitch reached the dog. The dog handler, faced with the suddenly triggered desires of his dog, had time only to shout once to get the car to move away from the wall before he was pulling madly at the leash to try to separate the animals.

In the nearest watch tower, a warden saw the two men run from the car towards the guard and the dogs and he laughed, amused by the sudden turmoil and sensing no danger in it. When he saw the two reach the guard and all three of them clump together he merely assumed, because of what had happened, that the two dogs had between them knocked all three together. He even saw the guard collapse to the ground without taking alarm – indeed, when the dog mounted the bitch he thought it so amusing that he picked up the telephone to speak to the switchboard operator and share the joke.

The carillon sounded. There was a half second's pause and then the first note of the hour struck. One road away, a man in the Rover closed the circuit on a radio transmitter.

The explosion was violent and the wall was shattered for a length of fifteen feet. A boiling cloud of dust and debris speared up into the air and then rained down while almost all the windows of the houses along Rowley Avenue were blown in or sucked out, depending on the vagaries of the explosion. A woman began to scream. The two Alsatians, after a brief pause of surprise, resumed what they had been doing before.

The Rover and the Vauxhall turned into Rowley Avenue, crunched their way over shattered bricks and came to a rocking halt in front of the gap torn in the wall. As they stopped, Thomas came through the gap, followed by the others.

Whistles began to blow and there was a rising tide of shouting. A fifth prisoner tried to tag along and Jenkins paused long enough to hit him brutally to the ground.

Thomas and Chase got into the Rover, Brent and Jenkins into the Vauxhall. The cars moved off to where Venables and Halliwell stood, momentarily stopping to pick them up, and then accelerated away. Immediately, the newly released men began to get out of prison denims into casual sports wear.

The first change-over was not as smooth as they would

have liked because a crowd of children were playing football quite close to the two get-away cars. Several pairs of ever-curious eyes watched them and they could be certain the police would get fairly accurate descriptions of their new cars. Twenty seconds after they'd driven off, the Rover and the Vauxhall burst into flames and burned so fiercely that the tarmac under and around them melted. The entranced children could move no closer than fifty yards to the blazing vehicles. Four minutes after that, the first patrol car roared round the corner.

The get-away cars left Mimblesham on the Cheddington road which was dual carriageway all the way, allowing them to drive quickly. When they reached the end of the dual carriageway they had seen no signs of pursuit and soon after entering the built-up area they passed a stationary patrol car, the occupants of which took no notice of them.

They parked behind a supermarket. The two drivers had been wearing gloves, yet even so they carefully wiped down the steering-wheels and any other surfaces which might have taken prints. When he was satisfied the cars were clean, Venables led the way round the side of the supermarket and along the narrow street, in which history and modern traffic did constant battle, to the parked Volvo and Ford. As the doors were unlocked, each man tensed because there was just one chance in a thousand that the police would have been lucky enough to outwit them and to have staked-out the two cars. But everything remained quiet.

As they drove out of Cheddington on the London road and passed the derestricted sign, Thomas laughed. 'It's the most expensive car ride I've ever made but, by God! it's been worth every penny.'

Rook sat at the desk in his fifth-floor office in the high-rise concrete-and-glass divisional H.Q. He picked up a pencil and doodled on the sheet of paper in front of him, eventually writing R.I.P. He wouldn't be called on to face an enquiry because his negligence hadn't been all that clear-cut (And how could he be charged without Mellon becoming equally involved?), but the entries in his confidential file would make it certain he gained no further promotion.

He stabbed the pencil down on to the paper, breaking off the point. He'd been so tired his mind had been filled with cottonwool. Even so, he'd handled the siege exactly as laid down. All the hostages had been saved. If three hundred thousand pounds had been lost, how small a proportion was that of the total capital which had been held in the bank?

He suddenly cursed Young. Why hadn't he smelled a rat when he'd handed over the suitcase marked A. R. Parsons? A good detective ought instinctively to know when he was dealing with a villain, yet Young had suspected nothing.

The internal telephone buzzed and Communications told him that news had come through of a prison break from Mimblesham Jail: Thomas, Jenkins, Chase, and Brent, had escaped.

He dropped the pencil on to the desk.

.   .   .   .   .

It was one in the morning and they'd arrived a couple of minutes before at the house which Drude had rented in Yexton and in which they'd stay until the hue-and-cry had died right away.

Thomas went over to the table on which Drude had just placed the suitcase and the others crowded round him. Each man checked the seals to see none had been broken.

'Here's a knife,' said Drude. He passed it across.

Thomas cut through the twine lashings and pulled them free. He pressed open the locks. Then, he flung back the lid.

Thomas reached forward and began to throw out the papers and files. 'It's the wrong case,' he shouted. 'That goddamn fool got the wrong bloody case.'

Drude knew one thing for certain – if he'd given Dutch Keen the wrong instructions, they'd kill him. 'You said the case was marked Parsons. That's what Dutch had to sign. This case is marked Parsons.'

Thomas jerked back the lid and saw that on the white label, in capital letters, was the name A. R. Parsons, written by himself.

'That bastard, Dutch, switched cases on us,' shouted Chase.

'Not the case, the contents,' corrected Thomas violently.

I I

Steen spoke to Wraight on Monday afternoon, after the bank had been shut to the public. He checked through the small spy-hole in the door to make certain Wraight

88

was not engaged, then knocked, opened the door and said: 'May I have a word with you, please?'

'Yes, but make it as brief as you can.' Wraight indicated a mass of papers on his desk. 'I've a great deal of work to complete.'

Steen brought out a letter from the breast pocket of his coat. 'I've just received this from my uncle. He was my father's brother and he left home some fifty years ago. There'd been no word from him until very recently, so I believed him dead. Then a letter arrived.'

Wraight looked impatient.

'He wrote to ask what had happened to the family and I told him I was now the only direct member living. This second letter which came this morning is asking me to go and see him so we could at last meet. I was wondering if I could have the two days' leave due to me and go to Mallorca for a long weekend?'

'We're very busy at the moment, as you must know.'

'Yes, I do, Mr Wraight, but he says he's not well and reading between the lines I reckon he's in rather a bad way – I think he wants to see me before it's too late. Would you like to read his letter?'

Wraight shook his head and began to tap on his desk with his short, stubby fingers. 'When do you wish to go?' he asked finally.

'As soon as possible.'

'Very well. But no more than the two days extra that you're due.' He pulled a folder across the desk to show the interview was at an end.

'There's just one more thing. I'm afraid I haven't very much money in my account and flying over at such short notice means I'll have to go schedule. Do you think I could have an overdraft to cover the fare?'

Wraight tapped on his desk once more. 'You know that

the rules for employees of the bank are quite clear – no overdrafts under normal circumstances. . . . However, the circumstances being what they are, I feel an exception is justified. I shall want you to pay it off within six months.' He made a brief note on his pad. 'The maximum will be a hundred and fifty pounds.'

'Thanks. I think it's going to mean a lot to Uncle Silas.'

'Silas?' said Wraight. 'That is not a Christian name one hears very often these days.' His tone of voice suggested that he considered the name an undesirable one.

Steen left. He wondered if he were the first person ever to ask for an overdraft of a hundred and fifty pounds when he had two hundred and seventy-five thousand pounds in cash. But then by doing just that he'd established the apparent fact that he was very hard up.

.   .   .   .   .

'Can you remember how your father said he got on with his brother?' asked Penelope, as she carefully packed Steen's suitcase on Thursday night.

'Father hardly even spoke about Silas. There were five years between them and there were such ructions over the disgraced maid that I reckon Father, who was only sixteen at the time, was brain-washed by his father into believing Uncle Silas had disgraced himself beyond redemption. . . . I wouldn't mind betting, though, if they'd ever met again it would all have been over and done with immediately.'

'It's so nice to think of his writing to you and wanting to see you now – after all, he's never even met you.'

'Does it do your sentimental soul good?' he teased her.

'Of course. And why not? . . . There! ' she stood upright. 'You've everything from casual wear to a dark suit, so you'll be able to fit in with whatever style he's living. Wouldn't it make a wonderful weekend if he has one of those fabulous villas one sees in the glossies?'

'It certainly would.' He was silent for a few seconds, then he said: 'I'm his only direct relative. So if he is well off, he might . . .' He did not finish the sentence.

'Bill, you know what I think of counting on wills before they're probated.'

'I don't see there's any harm in a good old day-dream. He isn't married and hasn't any children – we think – so he might leave me his all and that could be enough to let us go out and live in the sun so that your asthma and bronchitis become only a nasty memory.'

'Are you going to see him because you hope there's a chance of that happening?'

'I suppose if I'm honest I've got to admit the thought's there. But I'm really going because when a person's old and wants to see what's left of his family before he pops it, it doesn't seem much of a sacrifice on my part to go out. If I can make him a little happier, why not?'

She came round the bed and kissed him. 'You sometimes try to make out you're a cynic, but at heart you're just a wonderful old-fashioned sentimentalist.'

He knew a moment's guilty conscience because of the undeserved praise.

She looked at her watch. 'I'd better rush now or I'll miss the meeting.'

'Why not try to? From what you say it sounds as if you have to spend your entire time listening to all those old bitches rowing.'

'And they think you're so charming and polite! . . . I'll be back as soon as I can be, darling.' She kissed him goodbye and left.

He crossed to the east-facing window and watched her round the house and walk towards the car which he'd left outside the garage. God willing, within the next few months they would have moved to the sun and she would always walk tall and proud as she was now.

When the car had driven out on to the road, he carried the suitcase through to the studio. After removing some of the clothes, he packed in the bottom as much money as would fit, making certain not to include any of the twenty-pound notes. A bank customer had once told him how easy it was to smuggle currency out of the country. He hoped that customer had been right.

.   .   .   .   .

Val Thomas stubbed out a cigarette in the ash tray. He stared across the dining-room at Drude, his face harsh with anger. 'He can't just bloody disappear.'

Drude, not scared of Thomas but prepared to be wary of him, said: 'He must have put the skates under himself the moment he heard you'd been sprung from the nick.'

That, thought Thomas, was obvious. But Dutch was an alcoholic and with two hundred and seventy-five thousand pounds to spend he was probably on the biggest bender in history, all thoughts of self-preservation drowned in the booze. 'Move around the pubs.'

'I've been moving. There's no sign.'

'Keep moving. Try every town within reach.'

Drude turned and left the room.

Thomas slammed his clenched fist down on the table. Taken for two hundred and seventy-five grand by an old soak. . . .

.   .   .   .   .

The double-decker drew up outside terminal number two at Heathrow. Steen waited until the other passengers had moved, then he stood up and followed them down the stairs. The conductor had already opened the trailer and begun to unload the luggage and his suitcase was on the pavement.

There were thirty-two thousand pounds in that suitcase. If the Customs suddenly held a spot check on outgoing baggage, he was a dead duck.

He picked up the suitcase and carried it along the pavement and into the checking-in area. As he joined the queue of people he heard a couple argue about whether or not the gas in their home had been turned off. Too late now to worry, he thought. It was almost too late for him to worry, yet he was worrying until he sweated.

He reached the counter and lifted his suitcase up on to the scales. The needle spun round to record just under twenty kilos. A destination tab was stuck on to the handle and then the uniformed porter lifted up the suitcase and put it on the conveyor belt. The checker-in handed him back his ticket.

He moved away, but still watched the suitcase until it was out of sight. He imagined a few of the things which could happen now – the staff pillaging it, the strap caught on something and the lid torn off to scatter the contents all over the place. . . .

He went up the stairs and wandered along the general area, buying a newspaper at one of the kiosks. He read the headlines, but seconds later had no idea what they'd said: all he could concentrate on was that suitcase.

The emmigration officer looked at his passport, looked at him, then handed back the passport. No questions about currency. He carried on into the departure lounge and when he saw the bar he went over and bought himself a gin and tonic: it hardly seemed to moisten his mouth.

His flight was called. He went out of the departure lounge and along passages until he reached the security check, where he and the other passengers were frisked. Beyond was the sloped walk down to their embarkation point. As he waited halfway along this, he could look through a window and see their plane. A trailer, piled high with luggage, came round. He tried to identify his suitcase, but couldn't. Perhaps by some irony it had been left behind. . . .

They boarded.

The flight was uneventful and beyond the centre of France the sky was clear of clouds. They came in over the east of the island and the northern mountain range provided a dramatic approach of cliffs and barren moon-like surfaces.

After circling the airport once, they landed. Buses took them to the buildings and in the short walk up the path into the arrival area he was vaguely aware that the sun was hot and the flower beds were a riot of contrasting colours, but his thoughts centred on the suitcase. He handed in the immigration card and went to show his passport, but the immigration official waved him on.

In the arrival lounge the public-address system said, first in Spanish, then in English, that their luggage would be coming through at number one point. The looped conveyor belt began to move, bringing the luggage. Standing halfway down on the 'in' side of the endless loop he was able to see each piece of luggage as it came into sight and after five minutes he identified his suitcase and when it reached him he scooped it up. He walked down the length of the area, towards the armed Customs who stood by the check points by the large doors. There was a

94

stream of passengers and the two Customs seemed dis-
interested in anyone. He walked out into the long passage
which connected with the rest of the building. He was
through.

.　　　.　　　.　　　.　　　.

The bank stood on the corner of Calle Jaime de Navarra,
a kilometre from Palma Cathedral. One of the counters
was free and Steen crossed to it. 'Do you speak English?'
he asked the cashier.

'A little, Señor,' replied the other, voice thickly
accented.

'I would like to change some English money. Rather a
lot of money.'

The man nodded.

Steen took the thin wads of five and ten pounds notes
from his pocket and passed them over. Would the cashier
be surprised to be asked to change a thousand pounds in
notes?

'Passport, Señor, please.'

He panicked, then realized he was being ridiculous –
this must be routine. The cashier put the passport down
on the counter and counted the notes. He wrote the total
on a form. 'Señor, go,' he said, pointing across the bank
to another counter. He handed back the passport.

Steen crossed to the paying-out counter and there
waited for over five minutes as the currency form made its
leisurely way along the twelve metres which separated the
two points. The second cashier switched on a small
calculating machine and rapidly tapped out numbers. The
machine printed out and the cashier tore off the form
which he passed to Steen, pointing out a space where it
was clear Steen had to sign. He then removed one of the
two duplicate pages and passed this back. He opened a

drawer and brought out a large number of thousand-peseta notes, bundled up in fives with the fifth note enveloping the other four. He paid Steen one hundred and twenty-one thousand two hundred and sixty pesetas, less commission.

Steen dropped the few coins into his coat pocket and stuffed the notes into his breast pocket. The cashier's lack of interest made it clear that the transaction had been quite unremarkable and that the British had been smuggling currency abroad for a long time. So what Steen had seen as a hurdle which might take some clearing had, like previous hurdles, turned out to be no hurdle at all.

    •   •   •   •   •

Bank of England regulations were explicit and mandatory: no Britisher might open a foreign bank account without its consent. Luckily for currency smugglers, foreign banks could not have cared less what the insular Bank of England decreed.

The cashier in the Caja de Ahorros said he'd be pleased to open an account for Señor Steen. Steen put the suitcase on the counter, opened it, and began to unload the pesetas. The cashier, as he counted the notes, showed no more amazement than if he had been opening a customer's account with a few thousand rather than three million eight hundred and eighty thousand, three hundred and twenty pesetas.

    •   •   •   •   •

Drude hurried into the house in Yexton which had, for Thomas, Chase, Brent, and Jenkins, become just as much of a prison – albeit a comfortable one – as the one from which they had escaped. He found them in the sitting-room, watching racing on the television. 'Val – I've found him.'

Thomas swung round in his chair. 'You've found Dutch?'

'He got picked up in Astonfield for being blind drunk. Some smart Alec of a mouthpiece managed to get him off with a suspended sentence and a fine.'

'So where's he now?'

'Back at his place.'

Thomas balled his powerful hands.

12

On their honeymoon Penelope and Steen had stayed in a family hotel in Puerto Llueyo and the beauty of the bay had so fixed itself in Steen's memory he had decided this would be the area in which they'd live. For once, a return visit proved not to be a terrible mistake. The large bay, fringed by mountains which were not overpoweringly high, water deep blue, free of a single high-rise hotel, remained as beautiful as ever and as he stood at the end of the eastern arm of the small harbour, close to the gangway of a large motor yacht, he thought that this was an enchanted land.

The hot sun brought out the sweat on his arms and the

back of his neck as he imagined Penelope standing by his side. She would enjoy living out here, not solely because of the better health she would enjoy. With a quick, enquiring mind, a light sense of the ridiculous, and no automatic respect for either wealth or position, she was never wholly happy with the circle of acquaintances they had at Scranton Cross because she found their standards so arbitrary and wrongly based. Out here, he sensed, there were no set standards – people were largely accepted for themselves, without reference to their bank balances or ancestors.

He half turned and stared along the row of yachts and motor launches which ferried people to the justly famous Murelona Beach and he saw a fisherman, gnarled, burned walnut brown by the sun, who was mending a net. He would have liked to paint that man because he sensed that in him were all the virtues and vices of a stubborn, peasant, island race. He wondered what the old man thought about the flood of tourism which had altered his, and every other islander's, life so dramatically? Did he still remember the poverty and hardship he had once known, especially after the Civil War when food had been in even shorter supply than during it? Had he had brothers and sisters who had suffered the full viciousness of that fratricidal conflict? If only he were a good enough painter to put these questions and their answers into the face of the fisherman. . . .

He walked back down the harbour arm, past the yachts, the ferries, the fishing boats, and the gnarled fisherman who worked the shuttle with tireless dexterity, to his rented Seat 600. He climbed in and drove through the Puerto and along the six kilometres to Llueyo, an old town whose narrow, pavement-less roads were far more suited to the donkey-cart than to the car.

The solicitor to whom he'd been recommended lived and had his office in a house in Calle Mayor whose stark, shuttered exterior gave no hint of the spacious, almost luxurious interior. A middle-aged, largely toothless woman opened the door to his ring and she asked him in Spanish – he presumed that was what she asked him – to wait on one of the velveteen covered chairs in the entrance hall which clearly did second service as a waiting-room. His wait was less than a couple of minutes. Cifret came out of the room immediately on his right, greeted him in English, and shook hands with Spanish enthusiasm. He then led the way into a long, rectangular room, filled to over-flowing with bookcases, filing cabinets, stacks of papers, an enormous desk, chairs, and a dusty, overgrown rubber plant.

For a short time, Cifret spoke generalities – how was Steen enjoying the weather? Had he been to Mallorca and Llueyo before? Where was he staying? Then he leaned back in his chair and said: 'And, Señor, you want to ask me some things?' His English was fluent, with a sharp American accent which Steen guessed to be mid-Western in origin.

'I've come to ask if you can do something for me.' Cifret had been referred to as a man as sharp as a razor who'd chase a peseta over the Himalayas. But would he be prepared to take legal risks? Steen studied the unlined face with the very old and knowing eyes. 'You know that in England we have a lot of currency regulations?' he asked, speaking as unspecifically as possible until he could be certain Cifret would be sympathetic towards his proposal.

Cifret smiled – the smile did not reach those aged eyes – as he said: 'Señor, most countries have many rules and regulations, but usually they are of no importance. If you wish some money from England to Spain it is easy. You pay pounds to my friend in England and I pay you pesetas here. All it costs you is ten per cent and it will take about a fortnight.'

'That's very kind of you, but it's not my problem. I already have the pesetas out here.'

'Then perhaps you wish the money back in England? You are not supposed to take the money out with you, but give me the pesetas and you will be given pounds from my friend in England. It is again ten per cent only.'

'What I want to do is to buy a house in this area.'

Cifret failed to conceal his irritation. 'But that is simple. I do not understand your trouble. You have the money, I know of many houses . . .'

'It must cost about two and a half million pesetas and it's to be bought in the name of my uncle. That is the problem.'

'But again there is no trouble. . . .'

'My uncle has been dead for a long time.'

Cifret shifted in his chair and he fidgeted with an old-fashioned, heavy silver ink-well. 'But if he is dead . . .' He held out his hands and shrugged his shoulders.

'What I propose is that my uncle owns the house for a little and then dies. Officially dies, that is.'

Cifret said nothing.

'You will write to me in England and tell me of his death. You'll also send me a copy of the will in which he leaves me all his property on the island.'

'When a man dies, señor, there are many papers to manage, especially when it is a foreigner.'

'Does that mean you can't handle them?'

Cifret pursed his lips. 'I would have troubles. But I am very used to troubles. There is something else you must understand. When a man dies there are taxes to be paid.'

'Yes, of course.'

'And the fees to arrange the house to be in your name would perhaps be considerable.'

'I expect they would.'

'Much money would be saved if you should buy the house in your name and do not worry about your dead uncle who is to die.'

'Perhaps I would much rather not save the money.'

Cifret picked up a pencil and wrote some figures down on the top sheet of his notebook. 'I will tell you again, señor, that when a foreigner dies on this island many papers have to be sent to Madrid. To get these papers ready when no one has died will be . . . Very complicated.'

'How much?' asked Steen bluntly.

Cifret was upset by so crude an approach, but he told himself that the English never had been noted for their finesse. If the house were to cost two and a half million . . . The Englishman did not look wealthy, but since when did the fattest pig look the most beautiful? . . . How illegal, how risky, how many backhanders would have to be paid out? . . . 'Just to obtain such papers, señor, might cost as much as . . . Five hundred thousand pesetas.'

●　　●　　●　　●　　●　　●

Penelope met him at the station, just beyond the barrier which was up on the complex built out over the tracks. She came forward and gave him a brief, chaste kiss on the right cheek, but her eyes were warm with a far more expressive love. 'How are you, darling?'

He linked his free arm with hers and together they

walked towards the stairs which led down to the car-park. 'As fit as a fiddle.'

'I must say you look terrific. I'm sure you've even got a tan.'

'That wouldn't be surprising since it was sunshine from start to finish.'

'And we've been having clouds and more clouds! Did you go swimming?'

'At every possible opportunity.'

They reached the foot of the stairs and crossed to the outside, opened doors. A taxi driver looked hopefully at them, but they passed him and crossed to their battered Ford which was double-parked.

'So you really enjoyed it?' she asked.

'What d'you think? Do you remember the bay?'

'Don't I just! Those nights with the moonlight cutting across and the reflection of all the shore lights jiggling in the water? The fishermen out in the middle with the lights on the stern of their boats, spearing octopuses, or whatever it was they were spearing . . . Is it still as beautiful, Bill, or have they ruined it with building?'

'Just as beautiful,' he said, as he opened the passenger door for her. 'I kept looking at it and thinking that if we were there together it would be dangerously like paradise.'

'Dangerously?'

Paradise was always dangerous, he thought as he walked round to the driving side of the Ford. He sat down behind the wheel. 'Uncle Silas turned out to be tremendous fun. He's got the same kind of ironic humour as Father had – in fact it was rather like meeting an older father except that Uncle Silas is almost bald.'

'I'm so glad you liked him. Was his house nice?'

'It's a modernized finca surrounded by orange and lemon trees and with a vine-covered patio. If you go upstairs and lean out of the window just far enough not to fall out you can see the bay: at the back of the house are the mountains which are just the right size and don't make one feel horribly insignificant.'

'You make me want to rush to take the next plane out there!'

He started the engine. 'Uncle Silas told me he was leaving me the place.'

She half turned in her seat and stared at him. 'Oh, Bill!' she exclaimed, in tones of wonderment. Then, being a practical woman, she added: 'He'll probably change his mind. Old people often do. And even if he doesn't, we couldn't afford to live out there.'

'I don't know. I've been thinking.' He drove off. 'He must be living on capital, so there'd probably be some of that left. If we sold our house we'd have a bit over after the mortgage was paid off and on top of that maybe I could make a little from my paintings. I was talking to Uncle Silas about you and how we'd give anything to move to somewhere like the island and he said I might quite easily make some money — there are lots of artists who live near Llueyo and there are two galleries which have art exhibitions all the year round. I went into one of them and I don't think my stuff is any worse than some I saw. It's just possible I could sell enough chocolate-box to help pay for our food.'

She spoke indignantly. 'Stop talking about your painting like that. It's good and if you really worked at it it would be very good. . . .' Her voice changed tone and became wistful. 'Bill, do you really think there's a chance that he'll leave the house to you?'

'Yes, I do. He's no other close relative. And we got on very well with each other.'

'So one day we might live there and I wouldn't be ill so often and I could do so much more?'

'I don't think that "one day" can be very far off. He's not been fit for some time and the specialist's diagnosed cancer.'

'Oh! The poor man.'

'He doesn't expect to live for more than a few months, but that doesn't seem to worry him very much. Either that or he's incredibly brave. He asked me if I'd go out and see him again. You wouldn't mind, would you, Penny, even if I had to try and soften up old Wraight again to increase the overdraft?'

'Of course I wouldn't. To think of him out there, on his own with no relatives to help. It's terribly sad.'

Poor Uncle Silas, he thought.

.   .   .   .   .

Thomas and Chase waited in the car, stolen that morning, in the Fox and Hounds car-park. A large horse chestnut tree grew in the corner and they had drawn into its shadow so that, despite the outside light on the side of the building, their features were virtually indistinguishable.

'How much has he poured down his throat?' asked Chase angrily.

'Not even he can have swallowed two hundred and seventy-five thousand quid's worth of booze.'

'I wouldn't have thought the bastard had it in him to do the switch.'

It was a point which had worried Thomas. Dutch Keen was probably not a courageous man, nor except when drunk was he a fool: yet only a very brave man or a fool would have switched that money. And even a very brave man or a fool would then surely have disappeared for good?

They became silent, each man deep in his own thoughts.

At closing time, half a dozen men left the pub, two of them coming round to the outside lavatory. They saw Dutch Keen stand immediately outside the saloon bar entrance to talk, with much arm waving, to a man who looked as drunk as he, then walk away with jerky strides which suggested he was having to concentrate on each step.

Chase climbed out of the car. Thomas drove out of the car-park and turned left, went past the bowls club and along the curving road which brought him to the east side of the common, a fifty-acre space crossed by two roads that were lined with trees. At the cross-roads which virtually marked the centre of the common he turned left and saw ahead of him the plodding figure of Keen and, behind him, Chase. Thomas slowed the car as he checked in the rear-view mirror, then came to a stop in the shadow of trees halfway between street lights.

Keen came level with the car. ' 'Evening, Dutch,' Thomas said.

Had he been sober, Keen would have taken fright, but he came to a swaying stop and stared at the car and Thomas with worried perplexity.

Chase reached Keen's side. 'Get in,' he ordered. He opened the back door.

'You're going to take me home? That's real good of you,' said Keen, with gushing pleasure. 'To tell the truth – not a word of a lie, eh? – I'm tired. Been working too hard . . .'

Chase pushed him and he sprawled forward, hitting his shin on the door sill. As he struggled up into a sitting position, he said: 'There wasn't any need to do that:

I've hurt my foot now.' He belched. Chase sat beside hir
'You know, there wasn't no need to push me like that.
hurt myself.'

'So we'll call a bloody ambulance.'

As Thomas drove off he heard Keen mumble somethir
and Chase's order to belt up.

They turned right.

'I live along the other way,' said Keen. 'I've got a roo:
in a house. Look, you go right there and you can cu
through.'

Thomas drove straight on. 'We've a drink or two line
up for you, Dutch. Thought you'd like to celebrate.'

'Always ready to celebrate, that's me. As I alway
say . . . But what are we celebrating?'

No one answered him and after a short while he drifte
off into a drunken stupor.

Beyond the common was the suburb of Deerling ar
this stretched to the outskirts of Techington. The
reached open countryside, beginning to green up aga
after the previous long, dry spell and four miles out can
to a small wood which backed a disused gravel pit. The
parked just inside the wood, in a natural clearing, ar
jerked Keen awake. He mumbled questions, seemed u:
perturbed when he received no answers, and followe
Thomas along the narrow ride.

There was some broken-down fencing over which the
scrambled and then, Chase and Thomas supporting hir
they went down a steeply sloping side of a pit to tl
water's edge.

When Keen saw the scummy surface of the water in tl
torchlight he spoke petulantly. 'You said we was goir
to have a drink to celebrate. We can't celebrate nothir
here. We need a drink to celebrate. . . .'

'Where's the money?' demanded Thomas, his voice vicious.

'Money? I thought it was you going to give me a drink. But if you want me to pay for the round . . .'

Thomas punched Keen in the stomach and he doubled up. Chase kicked him in the side and he collapsed into the water. Thomas grabbed his legs and twisted him over, to hold his head under water. Keen frantically tried to free himself, but couldn't.

After a while Thomas let go of Keen and he surfaced. He choked violently, green slime slithering down his face. 'What d'you do that for?' he demanded, with pathetic indignation. He dragged himself to his feet and clasped his stomach with his hands.

'Where's the money?'

'What money? What are you on about?'

'The money that was in the suitcase.'

His bewildered mind at last understood and with understanding came a delayed identification. 'You're . . . you're Val Thomas.'

'And I want the two hundred and seventy-five grand.'

He squelched his way out of the water. 'Why d'you belt me in the guts and near drown me?'

'Listen, Dutch, to begin with you was smart, a sight smarter than I reckoned on. And maybe you'd of stayed smart if we'd remained in the nick. Only we didn't and you got bloody dumb and stayed around.'

'But why should I . . . ?'

'D'you know what was in that suitcase?'

'If I'd known at the time, I wouldn't've done the job for five grand. . . .'

'So what was inside it when you handed it on?'

'You know as well as me. Two hundred and seventy-five . . .'

'A load of papers and files. It was a smooth, smart switch, Dutch.' Thomas paused, then added: 'Only like I just said, you got dumb when you stayed around.'

'I . . . I did a switch?' He laughed.

They hit him, kicked him, and held his head under water until he lost consciousness.

When he regained consciousness, Thomas said: 'I want that money, Dutch.'

He was on all fours, trying to vomit and not quite succeeding. He was bleeding from his mouth and he explored with his tongue a gap where a tooth had been kicked out. 'I didn't do no switch.' His words were slushy because of the state of his mouth.

They dragged him a little way up the bank and bound his wrists and ankles with electric-light flex. Chase then stamped on his stomach and as he opened his mouth to cry out, jammed a duster in it.

They worked with care, using a couple of gas-filled lighters. From time to time they ungagged him and asked him where the money was, but all he did was to croak out the same terrified, pain-racked, desperate denial that he hadn't the slightest idea where it was.

As their frustrated anger grew, their methods became cruder and after a couple of hours Keen died. They pushed his body under the scummy water and weighted it down with stones.

Chase cursed as he tried to dry himself. 'Who'd of thought he'd the guts to keep his trap shut?'

'Haven't you yet realized he didn't know what happened?' asked Thomas scornfully.

13

Thomas poured himself out a heavy whisky.

'If Dutch didn't know nothing . . .' began Chase.

'Belt up.'

There was so much hair-trigger anger in Thomas's voice that Chase, who seldom bothered about other people's feelings, shut up.

Thomas drank. From the start he'd wondered why Keen had been so stupid as to stay around after nicking a fortune and now he knew the answer: Keen hadn't nicked anything. All he'd got out of the job had been a grand and a messy death.

Who had the money? The press and TV had highlighted the theft of the three hundred thousand pounds from under the noses of the police and there had been several cartoons, including one of a P.C. making an arrest and the arrested man picking the P.C.'s pocket. Since the police's image had taken such a knock, it was certain they'd have spread the news far and wide if they'd recovered the money.

After the prison break, he and the others had examined the suitcase before opening it to check that the seals were intact. They had been. Yet the case had been opened. So one of the bank staff must have made the switch.

Whoever had the money now would be living it up rich and therefore would be identifiable as the thief. But how could they find out which one of the staff *was* living it up? None of the four of them dared to be seen around and Drude couldn't do the job on his own.

He suffered a longing to smash something. Months of

planning had gone west when a woman screamed. Now a last-minute stroke of genius had gone sour because of some miserable little bank clerk.

He poured himself another drink. There had to be some way of finding out who'd nicked the money. . . . After a time he began to realize there might be a way, provided only that he was ready to risk everything in one move.

■　　■　　•　　•　　•

Penelope had caught a summer cold and this turned into bronchitis and asthma. At first it seemed the attack was going to be a severe one, but then just in time the antibiotic gained control of the bronchitis and they both knew that for once luck had been with her.

'I wonder what it was like in the old days,' she said, as she lay on the settee in the sitting-room. 'When one reads of someone suffering from asthma – or anything else – one forgets how much worse things must have been for them.'

The attacks were becoming more frequent, Steen thought. So the time-table must be speeded up. After all, there were not now the potential risks which he had originally envisaged.

'I had an aunt who used to suffer from asthma quite badly. She had a puffer with a powder which smelled like a clothes drawer which hadn't been opened for a long time and she wheezed. I used to try and imitate the noise she made . . . Isn't one cruel when one's young?'

'At least it's not deliberate cruelty,' he replied. 'By the way, did I show you the letter this morning from Uncle Silas?'

She shook her head. 'You didn't mention it, but that's

not surprising, is it? With me *hors de combat* you had a terrible rush before you left for work. How is he?'

He searched his coat pocket and found the typewritten letter. 'I'd say he's quite a bit worse than when I saw him. Wants me to go out again as soon as I can.' He passed the letter across.

She read it through. 'He's become a bit muddle-headed in the middle, hasn't he? You know, Bill, I do so hate to think of him living on his own, getting iller and iller.'

'I'd say he'd prefer to be on his own until the last moment. Rather like the way an animal will creep away to die.'

She shivered. Being so warm-natured, when she was ill she needed contact with someone she loved.

'You read that bit about keeping the garden weeded and watered so that everything will be in order when it's mine?'

She nodded as she put the letter down in her lap. She nibbled her upper lip, then said uncertainly: 'Bill, I know you're eager to inherit the house so we can live there and my health will be better and it's not because you're greedy. . . . But don't rush to step into a dead man's shoes. That's bad luck.'

He smiled.

'All right, you can laugh at me for being superstitious,' she said, 'but it's fact. You always have to pay for what you get.'

'Penny, if Uncle Silas was a fit man I'd wish him years of life in that finca and I'd never stop to think what it would be like for us to live there. But he's ill and, as he told me, in quite a lot of pain. When things reach that stage, I always hope for a quick end for the person concerned to stop the suffering. So I can honestly hope entirely for his sake that it's quick and yet at the same time work out what that would mean for us.'

She turned to stare through the window. It was another cloudy day, with only the odd patch of blue sky: it had rained the previous night, rain was forecast for tomorrow, and the temperature was several degrees below normal. A thousand miles south the sun was shining, the sea was a dazzling blue, the cicadas were chirping day and night, bougainvillaea was providing slashes of brilliant pinks, reds, and mauves. . . .

'When it does come to me,' he said, 'I've no idea how much capital there'll be. Life won't be all roses.'

She looked back at him. 'Bill, stop worrying. If we ever do go there I'm not expecting half a dozen servants. Just so long as we've enough to eat and we're happy.'

'Maybe I'll find a regular market for my paintings.'

'Last time you talked about it you were quite certain you would. Why are you now being rather pessimistic?'

'Because my latest painting isn't doing very well.'

'Well of course it isn't, not with you worried about me and tensed up over Uncle Silas. But when everything's settled one way or the other you're going to start painting really good pictures, I know you are.'

'If I could sell a couple a month, that would make a difference.'

'Remember that painting you did of me? One day, all your paintings are going to be as good as that and people will queue up to buy them.'

He laughed. 'From poverty to fortune in double quick time.'

'And why not? Let's build hundreds of Spanish castles in the air.'

He stood up, crossed to the settee, and kissed her.

'There's only one castle I'm really interested in. That's the one you live in in the sun.'

She ran her forefinger down the side of his cheek. 'I wonder why I'm so lucky as to have you as a husband?'

What would she ask herself if she ever learned even part of the truth? he wondered.

．　　．　　．　　．　　．

Ever since the drive to overcome the inherent disadvantages of having separate and autonomous police forces in the country had led, among other things, to the regional crime squads, a small department at New Scotland Yard had been collating the facts of major unsolved crimes in the whole country, summarizing those facts, and sending out a news sheet twice a week to all metropolitan and county forces – this was in addition to, and not instead of, other means of communication. The Summary of Current Crime had the effect of bypassing inter-force rivalries or even sheer bloody-mindedness: important information now passed automatically from one force to another.

Rook sat at his desk on the second Monday in August and glanced through the latest Summary of Current Crime. As he stared at the close-typed pages, photographically reproduced, he thought about his summer holiday which had, for the third year in succession, had to be postponed. Mellon had said there was too much work outstanding for him to go away for a fortnight on the dates arranged. There was a lot of crime on the books of the division, but none which Young could not have handled for the time he was away. But Mellon, contrary to his appearance of bluff camaraderie, was vindictively minded, especially when someone else's actions touched his own career. Rook sighed. Amy had appeared to accept the news of the holiday cancellation philosophically, but her disappointment had been obvious.

He jerked his attention back to the present and read with more concentration. Murder, rape, extortion, attempted kidnapping, maiming, bombing. When one knew what inhumanities had happened one had to be a supreme optimist not to believe that the human race was beyond redemption. . . .

He came to an entry which immediately cut short his woolly philosophizing and sharpened his interest. Dutch Keen had been found, tortured to death, floating in a disused gravel pit. There was no known motive and enquiries had uncovered no suspects. He had a record of small convictions, mainly for confidence tricks. He had been an alcoholic. The final entry was a physical description.

Rook dropped the report on to his desk. People of Keen's background didn't get tortured to death unless they had information to give or were believed to have informed on someone, and in the latter case death was usually quick rather than prolonged because revenge made for hasty tempers. What information could he have had that was worth his death? His description suggested one possible answer.

Rook phoned the investigating force and spoke to a detective sergeant who gave him a fuller description than had been printed. Fiftyish, tall, well-built and lean, long face tanned, brown eyes, bushy eyebrows, Roman nose, full lips, false teeth, cleft chin, ears slightly winged, greying hair well tended . . .

After ringing off, Rook tried to call Young on the

internal phone, but there was no answer. Typical of the bloody man, he thought sourly.

. . . . .

'There's a couple of hundred nicker,' said Thomas, as he pushed the slim bundle of notes across the dining-room table.

'I don't like it . . .' began Drude.

'I don't remember asking you to.'

'If I chat up one of the civvy broads working for the coppers someone may begin to wonder.'

'You and me's never worked together before, so there ain't no tie-up. And when you joined the team you dropped out of sight like the rest of us so there ain't no nark can fink you. No one at the bank got a butchers at you.'

'There could be a copper knows my mug.'

'When you ain't never worked that part of the country?'

'They move around.'

'So what if someone looks at you and says to himself, Paul Drude? . . . You ain't wanted because no one knows the identity of the fifth bloke. You can spit in any copper's eye.'

'But my wife . . .'

'She's great. But you ain't going to feed me with the fairy story that you ain't humped anyone else since you was married.'

That didn't prevent his loving his wife and children. But it was impossible to explain his feelings.

'What's the real trouble, Paul? Things getting a little strong for you?' Thomas spoke with contempt. He stood up, kicked the chair backwards and crossed to the sideboard where he poured himself out a whisky.

Drude spoke angrily. 'All I'm saying is, it could be tricky.'

With a quick switch of emotion, Thomas suddenly sounded amused, not contemptuous. 'Tricky? With your technique?'

'It's got to take time, though. I can't rush it.'

'You're the expert.'

Drude fidgeted with the money. 'Val, a couple of centuries don't go far.'

Thomas, with calculated generosity, brought more money from his pocket and counted out another two hundred pounds. 'Don't splash it too hard, Paul – there ain't all that much left in the kitty now.'

Drude gathered up all the money. 'You don't think you could be wrong and it weren't no one in the bank made the switch?'

'No.'

'All right. But what if the coppers don't understand that Dutch was the bloke what got the suitcase from the bank? Then I ain't going to get anywhere with any broad.'

'The average split ain't a genius, but likewise he ain't a fool. They know Dutch was worked over before he bought it so they'll be asking themselves why. And they're going to come straight up with the answer that he'd information some villain wanted. That'll lead 'em to the bank job. The Scranton Cross splits will start asking. Dutch picks up the suitcase and takes it off and six weeks later gets himself murdered: what's the silly bastard been up to? Nicking all the lovely lolly for himself? But then they're going to think a bit harder. Dutch wasn't no hero – ten seconds with the cigarette lighter and he'd've sung like he was in Covent Garden. So it begins to look like there was a switch of the money and it was done by some-one in the bank. . . . That's when they're going to start checking on who's spending hard. And when they've got an answer, I want to know what it is, bloody quick.'

'It's a hell of a gamble.'

'So's life. Look, you work hard until she can't see Richard Burton for your lovely mug and she'll give you everything you want, including the news.'

'But the splits'll find out what's been going on as soon as you take out the bastard who did the switch. Then they're going to nail me for who I am.'

'Just like the four of us are nailed, Paul.'

Drude saw there was no way out of it, even though there was every probability that he would eventually be identified as the fifth bank robber.

. . . . .

Wraight rested his elbows on the desk and joined his fingertips together, then ran his thumbs backwards and forwards across his lips. 'Doing his Shylock imitation,' was how Gaitshead described it. He finally spoke. 'It's only a short time since you had several days off to visit your uncle, isn't it?'

'It was about a month ago, Mr Wraight,' said Steen, 'and as a matter of fact I was owed the extra days I had off. . . . As you can read in his letter, he's worse now than he was and he does ask me very strongly to go and see him. I'm afraid this may be the last chance.'

Wraight picked up a statement and studied it. 'I note that you've hardly begun to pay off the overdraft I allowed you for that first trip.'

'There's hardly been the time.'

'I asked you to clear the overdraft in six months, but you have not reduced it by one sixth.'

'Things are so expensive . . .' Steen sounded miserable. Then he cheered up. 'I could ask him to pay my expenses for this trip. I don't think he'd mind.'

'But clearly you won't be able to do that before you go so that inevitably you have to continue to ask to be temporarily allowed to increase your overdraft.' Having established the situation in its plainest terms, Wraight relaxed. He lowered his arms, and looked again at the statement before him. 'Very well, I will increase the limit to allow you to purchase a return fare to Mallorca. But I expect you to try and persuade your uncle to refund the amount.'

14

Puerto Llueyo brooded under a hot sun with a timelessness that reduced all clocks to impotence. Steen looked across the restaurant table at his dining companion. 'You were right about this restaurant.'

'The food, señor, is good and the scene is beautiful.' Vives was small and thin and his olive skin and very dark eyes suggested that more Moorish blood ran in his veins than in most Mallorquins.

Steen looked through the nearby window at the bay, stretched about them since the restaurant stood on the western harbour arm. He saw a power boat start up at full throttle to bring a water-skier upright, leaving gashes of white across the vivid blue. 'My wife's going to love living here.'

'But of course,' murmured Vives.

'And I reckon it'll do my painting a lot of good. There's so much colour.'

Vives scooped out the last two mussels from their shells, added some sauce to the spoon, and ate them. 'I will be very pleased, señor, to observe whatever you paint. But you will understand that I am not able to say that I will put in my gallery your paintings until I have seen them.'

'Obviously, you have to be fairly certain of selling what you show.' Vives, thought Steen, looked as sharply interested in money as Cifret. 'Suppose you could be certain every painting of mine would sell, would you hang it whatever you thought of it?'

Vives looked curiously at him, then lifted up his glass and drank some of the white Binissalem wine. 'It is so difficult to be sure a painting will sell.'

'But if you could be certain?'

Vives finished his wine and Steen refilled their glasses.

'May I explain something? My wife has an exaggerated belief in my ability as a painter. Because I'm vain enough to wish to justify her belief, even though I know it's unjustified, I want to make it appear that my paintings sell almost as soon as they reach the market. So suppose from time to time I gave you a painting and you hung it in your gallery for a short while and then took it down and reported it had been sold and paid me the selling price less your full commission, would that be a business proposition?'

'Señor, it would, but for one question. If the painting does not really sell, where does the buying price arrive from?'

'Me.'

Vives fidgeted with the stem of his wineglass. 'You will bring me paintings which I will cost, perhaps for ten thousand pesetas? After they are showing for some days I take them down and say they sell? You give me two thousand. Is this what you say?'

'Exactly.'

Vives was torn between the feeling that nobody could be quite so stupidly affectionate towards his own wife therefore this was far more complicated than it seemed, and the greedy desire to make money so effortlessly. In the end, his greedy desire won. 'Señor, it will be a pleasure to hang your paintings in my gallery.'

Steen stared out through the window once more. Now he could make certain that a small but regular income reached him with every appearance of legality.

The waiter brought them a pan piled high with Paella Valencia. He served them and added a final gamba on each plate with a flourish of serving spoon and fork.

'Would you like another bottle of wine?' asked Steen.

'Indeed. It is a very nice wine.' The tourist trade might be temporarily depressed, thought Vives, but there were still a few wealthy foreigners around to compensate for that fact.

.   .   .   .   .   .

Steen walked through the narrow, twisting streets of Llueyo to the Calle de la Huerta and Cifret's house. The middle-aged woman with her warm, toothless smile opened the outside wooden door and showed him into the entrance hall. He sat down and listened to a murmur of voices from the office.

After a quarter of an hour, Cifret came out of the office

with an elderly man. He smiled at Steen, escorted the man to the door and said goodbye in French, then returned and shook hands. 'Good afternoon, Señor Steen. You are well? It is very nice to see you again. Please to enter.'

Steen went into the office, slightly more cluttered up than before. 'I've come to find out how close you are to completing the purchase of the finca in my uncle's name?'

'It all takes time, as you will understand, señor, especially with things a little unusual. I have had to . . . How would you say? Imagine up a few details? And always Madrid wants more papers. But events are moving.'

'Then how soon do you reckon the purchase will be completed?'

Cifret looked at the perpetual calendar on his desk which was set at the wrong date. 'A week, or maybe a little longer. As there was no residencia, I had to discover a passport and that was rather difficult. . . . I have a friend who works in a hotel. . . .' His manner plainly said that the final bill was going to be a very steep one.

'You sorted out the problem of military permission?'

'I managed to persuade the military that your uncle's house was just outside the limits where he would need military permission to buy it. . . . Today it is easier to persuade people.'

'Then you really should be able to complete soon?'

'I am sure of it, señor.' He wasn't sure, but it was good manners to tell a person whatever that person wished to hear and in any case if it weren't completed soon, no doubt it would be completed later. . . .

'The moment everything's fixed up, I want you to kill off Uncle Silas.'

'I will do that, señor. A thought has come to me. Do you wish for a grave?'

'Yes, I do. My wife will almost certainly want to visit it to put on flowers.'

'It becomes difficult . . . But then I have a friend who will assist. Since five years ago, foreigners may be buried in the cemetery in Llueyo and so it will not be as difficult as if one had to arrange matters in Palma.' Cifret nodded complacently. 'There is one small matter I would like to talk about. I have paid several monies. Will you now give me some money?'

'How much?'

Cifret searched amongst the folders on his desk and eventually found the one he wanted. He opened it. 'It is eighty-five thousand and four hundred pesetas, señor.'

'What exactly does that cover?'

Cifret was a little disappointed since he had decided that Steen would not check the accounts. 'I shall write you the details, of course.' He smiled broadly. 'We are businessmen, are we not?'

Of a kind, thought Steen.

.   .   .   .   .   .

Young sat on the window sill in Rook's office. 'I've been on to the Techington police again and they've nothing new to offer. There's no motive they can trace. So that makes it certain we're right and there *was* a second switch of the loot in the bank. Dutch Keen thought he was carrying out the original, but in fact he'd only a load of junk. The suitcase obviously wasn't opened until Thomas and the rest of 'em had been sprung – they'd have been too suspicious of each other – and then they found the junk and not the fortune. They reckoned Dutch had twisted 'em.'

Certain? wondered Rook.

'So now we start in on the bank staff and find out who had the clever idea?'

Rook leaned his chair back until it touched the wall. He rested his feet on the desk. 'It's going to be tricky, especially with the senior staff.'

'I'm not scared of anyone in a bank,' said Young brashly.

'Nor am I, but that doesn't stop me being careful not to make mistakes. When you start dealing with people in their position you look twice before you leap or you end up in the midden.'

Young looked faintly scornful.

'I've met the manager socially; he's a Rotarian. I'd say he's the last bloke in the place to have lifted the money.'

'We forget him because he's a Rotarian?'

'Don't be so bloody silly. But we can afford to work through him. He'll know the staff because he's a fussy little man. If anyone's acting out of normal, he'll be aware of it.' Rook removed his feet from the desk and allowed the chair to crash forward. His voice suddenly sharpened. 'I want the bastard who made the switch nailed, and nailed fast.'

It'll be too late for your career, thought Young.

Rook stood up. 'We'll move along to the bank now and have a preliminary chat.'

'I've a hell of a lot of work on hand. . . .'

'It'll keep. . . . You know, I can't help thinking of that poor devil. All the time they were burning him he must have been desperate to tell them what they wanted, yet couldn't.'

Young shrugged his shoulders. He would never worry over someone like Dutch Keen.

The day was sultry, almost stormy in oppressiveness,

and the walk to the bank made both men sweat slightly. They entered and went down to the enquiries counter and asked to see Wraight. The woman they spoke to said he was engaged with a customer, but she'd ring and tell him the detectives were waiting to see him. Rook sat down at one of the small tables and picked up a pamphlet which told him how much interest he could earn himself merely by investing in a deposit account. Great news for those not on police salaries, he thought.

Wraight showed a beefy farmer-type out of his room and escorted him along the open passage and through the swing door. He said goodbye and then crossed to Rook. 'Sorry to have kept you waiting.'

'Sorry to break in on you unexpectedly,' replied Rook.

Wraight looked keenly at the D.I. 'Presumably something important has occurred? Let's go along to my room.' He led the way into his office.

When they were all seated, Rook said: 'Did you read the other day about a man called Dutch Keen who was found murdered in a gravel pit? He'd been tortured to death.'

'Yes, I did. A truly horrible affair. As I said to my wife, things just get worse and worse. What on earth could make anyone do a terrible thing like that?'

Rook told him.

Wraight sat very upright in his chair and he spoke with sharp dignity. 'That is quite impossible! No member of my staff would ever do such a thing.'

'Why not?' asked Young.

'Because they are honest.' Wraight noticed the look on Young's face. 'You clearly do not understand. The people who work here are completely trustworthy or they would not be here. I will personally guarantee every one of them.'

Rook, hurrying to forestall any comment from Young,

said: 'I appreciate your strong feelings, Mr Wraight, but strange things can happen.'

'But damn it, they're surrounded by money all their working lives! It doesn't mean a thing to them. If someone had found this money in a suitcase, he'd immediately have reported the fact. A suitcase full of money couldn't tempt any of us.'

'Frankly, I've thought about that aspect of things and it does worry me.'

'Well, then . . .'

'But we can't uncover any reasonable motive for Keen's murder other than that the bank mob were trying to get information out of him as to where the money had got to.'

'You are supposing a very great deal.'

'In a way, yes, but it's all pretty logical supposition.'

'Which could be very wrong, however logical it seems.'

'Of course.'

'I am quite certain it is wrong, for the reasons I've given.'

'Your opinion obviously means a lot, Mr Wraight, but I'll still have to check up.'

Wraight flushed, as if it had been his own honour which had been impugned. 'What exactly do you mean by "check up"?'

'If there was a switch, I want to know who were in a position to have made it. Then the lives of those people will have to be checked to see if any of them has suddenly started to spend. . . . Who amongst the staff was down in the strong-room after the raid and before the bank reopened?'

'I was.'

Rook smiled easily. 'I should have added, excluding yourself.'

Wraight drummed on the desk with the fingers of his

right hand. 'Seebring and Hodges checked out the notes. Steen handled the valuables.'

'And no one else went down to the strong-room until the suitcase in the name of Parsons was withdrawn?'

'I am not prepared to say that, although I know of no one. As you know, most of the staff remained at home all that Friday. But surely those three will tell you if they saw anyone else down there?'

'Yes, but I have to cross-check. Mr Wraight, am I right in thinking it's a rule that all staff members have to bank with their branch of the bank?'

'You are correct.'

'Then may we see the bank statements of Seebring, Hodges, and Steen, to find out if there's been any change in spending?'

'You need a court order for that.'

'Officially, yes. But that would be to bring the whole thing out into the open, wouldn't it, and the result might not be too good for the bank's image. Do it quietly and if we find nothing no one outside of us three will ever know what the suspicions were.'

Wraight again drummed on the desk with his fingers.

'You'll guess the kind of thing we'll be looking for – a regular sum used for housekeeping which suddenly isn't drawn, a deposit that doesn't fit the person's salary.'

'I can assure you that none of them has deposited three hundred thousand pounds.'

Rook smiled, missing the point that it had not been intended as a joke.

Wraight hesitated a little longer, then used the internal phone to ask for the staff statements to be brought in to him. In less than a minute a woman carried in a large folder, thick with papers. She glanced around with quick curiosity before putting the folder down on the manager's desk and leaving.

Wraight checked through the papers and withdrew three sheets. 'There you are. The last statements, covering six months and up to date a fortnight ago.'

Rook studied the figures. In Seebring's and Hodges's cases the pattern of deposits and withdrawals was regular, before and after the bank raid: Steen's figures showed the sudden overdraft, recently increased. 'Do you know why Steen went into the red?'

'Of course. No member of the staff is allowed an overdraft without my express permission. Steen has an uncle who now lives in Mallorca but who seems to have roamed the world for a number of years after leaving home in disgrace. The uncle wanted to see Steen, who's his sole remaining blood relative, and asked him to go out to the island. He hadn't the money to pay for the fare and asked me if he might have the initial overdraft. I allowed it. Then he came to me on Tuesday with a second letter from the uncle, asking him to go out again – in fact, he's travelling today. I gather from the tone of the letter that the uncle has little time to live. As this was a compassionate ground I allowed the increased overdraft.' He said, very dryly: 'If Steen had helped himself to hundreds of thousands of pounds, I doubt he would have come to me to ask for the overdrafts.'

'Probably not. . . . He was working on his own, wasn't he, when he was sorting through the valuables?' He turned to Young. 'How was that suitcase secured?'

'With white twine and seals,' replied Young immediately. 'I can't say if it was locked because I didn't test the locks.'

'Have you any idea what the seals were?'

'No.'

Rook rubbed his chin, then spoke to Wraight once more. 'The villains seem to have been able to open the suitcase and then reseal it – when they collected it, it was either as they'd left it or, if there was a switch, the person who did that switch must have fixed up the case as near as possible to how it had been. Since the mob wouldn't have known they were going to do this, there must surely be seals, twine, and sealing-wax readily available?'

Wraight spoke a shade stiffly. 'I thought I'd answered that previously? . . . The regulations call for all sealing-wax and seals to be held under close security. Probably there's a seal and sealing-wax down in the strong-room so that they're handy when they're wanted, but since normally nowhere could be more secure it is not a practice I have ever checked, in either sense of the word.'

Rook visualized the strong-room as he had last seen it. 'The shelves come out from the walls to make a rough enclosure, don't they? And when they're filled with cases it can't be all that easy to see into the enclosure?'

'Well?'

'Seebring and Hodges were busy checking the money, but even if they'd tried to look it wouldn't have been easy for them to see what Steen was doing?'

'I wish to say this. William Steen has worked in this bank for some eight years and in that time he has proved himself to be intelligent, competent, and trustworthy. And since it seems necessary to do so, I repeat, had he stolen all that money would he ever have come to me to ask for an overdraft?'

Yes, if he were clever enough to foresee the posibility of an investigation into his financial position, thought Rook.

Steen arrived at Scranton Cross station on Monday evening and Penelope was waiting for him by the ticket collector. He kissed her on the cheek and then went down the stairs and out to their battered old Ford.

As soon as they were seated, she asked: 'How was he?'

'Looking groggy, but amazingly cheerful. I reckon he's one of those people who genuinely isn't worried about dying. In fact, he said that he'd be sorry to lose me after only just meeting me, but he didn't give a button about saying goodbye to anyone else . . . Then he winked and added you in along with me, even if he hadn't actually met you.'

'It's rather sad and yet cheering, isn't it, that he can talk like that?' She was silent until he had driven out of the car-park. 'I don't suppose you knew, but we've had terrible weather whilst you were away. What kind have you had?'

'The sun only stopped shining at night. It got so hot I even had a siesta on Sunday.'

'What decadence! I can see that if we ever do live out there I'm going to have to work hard to stop you going completely bush.'

'Then you'd better start girding your loins. I don't think it'll be very long.'

'I'm all excited at the thought and yet also a little scared. Is that being stupid?'

'I don't see why – it'll be a hell of a change.'

'And an adventure, especially for people like us. I mean, we're so ordinary and ordinary people don't usually pick up their sticks and leave their country. I keep wondering how I'm going to cope with shopping. I've tried to learn Spanish for the usual things and all I succeed in doing is getting them hopelessly muddled.'

He laughed. 'Shopping's obviously going to be interesting.'

'Did you ask anyone whether there's much asthma?'

'A retired English doctor confirmed that the locals get it, but foreigners who suffered from it back in their own countries are usually much better off on the island. It's probably a case of escaping from whatever triggers it off and not finding that something on the island.'

'I don't care how many times I make a fool of myself in the shops, or how many dowager duchesses condescend, if only I can stay fit. . . . I still don't believe it can really come true.'

'It'll soon come true,' he promised her.

. . . . . .

There was an air of brash, hard self-confidence about Paul Drude which attracted a certain type of woman and generally speaking such women were unperturbed when they recognized a little of the vicious toughness in his character.

Hazel Neeve was averagely intelligent, averagely sophisticated, and quite attractive. She thought Drude handsome and liked the way he wasn't scared of anyone, not even of head waiters. She was also very impressed by the way he spent money: all the men who had previously taken her out had had to watch the pennies, he had a careless disregard for the pounds.

On Wednesday, he took her to a dance at the Hotel Olympic, in Nuncton, a seaside resort long noted for its high proportion of resident retired officers. The hotel was on the front and had such an imposing façade, and the two doormen were so smart in their light grey uniforms, that she was a little bit scared and wondered if her dress was smart enough. The prices on the menu scared her even more.

Drude ordered and they drank a bottle of champagne and then ordered another. They danced in between courses and he told her that he had never danced with anyone so beautiful and she believed him and felt wonderfully happy. She drank more champagne to celebrate her happiness and giggled when she discovered that her feet kept becoming slightly mixed up.

Later, after the staff had been tipped to their evident, if superior, satisfaction they left and began the drive home. Up in the hills he stopped and she had just time to warn herself to be careful when he started to kiss her with a skill she hadn't previously experienced. Before long, she forgot her own good advice.

15

Rook walked into Young's office. There was a large calendar on the wall showing a nude blonde who was preserving her final secret by only a millimetre. Rook stared at her.

'That's Olive,' said Young. 'She makes old men young and young men frantic. So how frantic are you?'

Smart alecky bastard, thought Rook, as he sat down on

the edge of the desk. 'How's the work coming along in the bank job?'

'One of the girls is typing out my report now. I was going to bring it along as soon as it's ready.'

'Let's have a quick summary. Have you got anywhere?'

'The pattern's the same for the three of them. They all live in houses which were bought on money borrowed from the bank . . . By the way, did you know they still get a mortgage at a rate well below the commercial one?'

'Some people are born lucky.'

'They run tired cars, their tired wives dress at Marks and Sparks, they drink beer when they can afford it and water when they can't, and if any of 'em's got three hundred thousand tucked away, he hasn't yet started to use it.'

Rook swore to himself. Careful cross-checking had shown that only Steen had really been in a position to switch the contents of the suitcase (assuming it had been switched), but Seebring and Hodges had been working in the strong-room when on their own so that the possibility of their having done the job together had to be remembered. Since none of their bank statements had shown any significant variation from normal (apart from Steen's overdrafts) and there were no obvious signs of sudden affluence, each man would have to be interviewed in his own home. And if that proved negative . . . Then it must seem likely that the contents of the suitcase had not been switched, that the murder of Dutch Keen was unexplainable, that there was little hope of recovering the stolen money. His future, thought Rook, was beginning to look as if it would remain bitched up.

.   .   .   .

Early Thursday evening Steen was in the sitting-room, watching the news on the television, when he heard a car drive in. He stood up and crossed to look through the window and he saw a grey Marina.

Penelope, who was upstairs, called out: 'Who's that, Bill? It isn't Noreen, is it? I promised to go to one of her awful coffee parties this morning and clean forgot all about it. If it is her, you'll have to help me.'

'I'm just on my way out for a long, long walk.'

'Coward!'

He saw two men climb out of the car and recognized them as they approached the corner of the house. He felt as if someone had dropped a couple of hundredweight of ice into his stomach. True, the detectives had recently been to the bank and spoken to Wraight, but everyone had assumed that this had been a purely routine visit, probably the last they would make. Yet now . . . Why should they come to the house? . . . How could this be routine?

'Bill, it's two men, not Noreen.'

'They're the detectives.' He heard the front gate squeak open, then seconds later squeak shut. He wanted to run and hide.

There was a knock on the front door.

'Bill, aren't you going to see what they want?'

He went into the hall and opened the inner door to the porch.

Rook said: ' 'Evening, Mr Steen. Sorry to disturb you like this, but I had to come along and check up on one or two things. You know Detective Sergeant Young, of course?'

Young nodded.

'Come in,' said Steen.

They entered and Rook looked up at the apex of the hall. 'What a wonderful old house! It's my wife's ambition to live in a house like this, all beams and old plaster – someone once told me the old plaster used to be made up of straw, mud, and dung. Could that be right?'

Rook's manner was so easy and friendly that Steen became certain his sudden fear had been totally unnecessary: yet again, a guilty conscience had distorted events. 'I've always understood that those were some of the ingredients. This house isn't nearly as old as its name suggests, but we've got bits of wall still of the old plaster and that's certainly got straw in it.'

Penelope appeared at the head of the stairs and came down.

Steen introduced her to the detectives.

'I've just been admiring your house,' said Rook, 'and telling your husband that it's my wife's ambition to live in one like it.'

'We like it very much, even if it does cost so much in upkeep.' She smiled a trifle shyly because what she was about to say often, she felt certain, sounded like nonsense to insensitive people. 'But it's so wonderful to know one's living in a little bit of history.' She smiled again. 'My only trouble is, I get my history so wrong. I became all excited when I thought I'd discovered a priest's hole up in the attic, behind the central chimney-stack – then I checked up on dates. But at least there've been two hundred years of people living in it and although I don't suppose any of them ever did anything famous, they've been part of the country . . . Would you like to look over it? I'm afraid it's a bit untidy in Bill's studio, but I never go and clean up in there.'

'I'd love to look around, Mrs Steen.' He half turned. 'I didn't know you painted, Mr Steen.'

'Only in a small and very amateur way.'

'Not so small and not so very amateur,' she said

stoutly. 'And it's going to become in a big professional way when we're living in Mallorca.'

Rook could not contain his surprise.

She noticed his expression, but misinterpreted it. 'We hate the thought of leaving this house, of course. If only we could pick it up and drop it down over there. But then perhaps the sun would dry everything right out and it would fall down. . . . Come on upstairs.'

They went upstairs, in single file. As they entered the main bedroom, Rook said casually: 'When did you decide to move?'

She seemed not to have heard the question. 'D'you see the way the beams go in the corner over there? I always called them dragon beams until we had a friend to stay who claimed to know a lot about old houses and he told us that dragon beams were much older and these could only have been put in as imitation. Now I call them dragonet beams.'

Rook laughed politely. Young looked bored.

Steen hastened to explain their coming move. 'A bit over a month ago a long lost uncle wrote from Mallorca and asked me to go over there and see him. We got on rather well together and he told me that as he was very ill and I was his only blood relative, he was going to leave me his property. If he does, we're going to try living out there to see if the island helps Penelope's asthma and bronchitis.'

'And Bill's going to paint lots of pictures and make a fortune,' she added.

'I'm sorry to hear you have asthma and bronchitis so badly,' said Rook. 'I certainly hope the move does you a world of good.'

'It's still a case of if we make the move,' said Steen

hurriedly. 'You know what elderly relatives are like – one day you're the heir, the next the cat's home is.'

'So I've often been told. But as far as I'm concerned, if I've a relative who could leave me anything but debts, I've never heard about him.'

'It'll probably turn out to be the cat's home in our case,' said Penelope, 'and we'll continue living here. I'll just have to tell myself even harder not to be so silly as to get worked up over anything.' She walked back to the door. 'Come on through to the studio, but don't forget that I warned you it may be terribly untidy.'

They saw the rest of the house and Rook was lavish with his praise, some of which was genuine.

In the sitting-room, after he had poured out four beers, Steen said, in tones more challenging than he had intended: 'You want to question me?'

Rook shook his head. 'I didn't say question you – that's all very formal. All I want to do is check up on a few details.' He leaned back in the armchair and crossed his legs with every appearance of being completely at ease. 'I'd like to go over that Friday again . . . I know you've repeated the facts until you're sick and tired of them, but there could just be something small you've forgotten which might give us a new lead. . . . I'll be frank, if we don't get a new lead, we'll have had it.'

'You won't be able to trace the men or the money?'

'I'd say that eventually we'll get the men, but by then the money will all have gone.'

'Surely it'll take them ages and ages to spend that fortune?' asked Penelope.

'Not really, Mrs Steen, because it's not as simple as perhaps it appears. They've three hundred thousand, less what it cost them to fix the prison break, but everyone knows they've got it. Anyone who's hiding them is going to grab as big a piece of that cake as possible, any-one who knows where they are is going to put the screws on them. . . . There is no honour among thieves when there's money around: it's every man for himself and let the devil cut the throat of the last one.'

'How horrible. I mean, if there were honour there'd at least be something worth while about them.'

'I'd not go that far. Still, it makes our job a lot simpler to have things as they are. . . . Now, Mr Steen, if you'd go over all the details again?'

Three-quarters of an hour later, the detectives left.

Penelope said: 'What nice people, Bill. Not at all like I imagined a detective was.'

Had Rook's surprise at the news of their coming move developed into suspicion? Not, Steen told himself, if one judged by his attitude throughout their visit. But was it safe to accept that at face value? To hell with the ques-tions. The detectives could never uncover the truth.

    .   .   .   .   .

They drove back through the lanes towards Scranton Cross.

'If he swiped the loot he hasn't spent any of it on the house,' said Young, with some scorn. 'The telly was black-and-white and that carpet in the main upstairs bedroom was worn right through in the centre.'

One day – perhaps – Young would discover that there were more important things in life than coloured television and new carpets, thought Rook briefly. 'But he has found a long-lost uncle who's decided to leave him a house.'

'You reckon there can be anything in that?'

Rook drove carefully around a corner. 'When I checked

his bank statement I discovered he'd been given two overdrafts. I spoke to Wraight about them. That first overdraft was dated after the bank raid, something like a month ago.'

'I don't see how that can be anything but a coincidence.'

'I don't like coincidences which are too convenient. And another thing. It's been difficult to visualize someone of Steen's character and background suddenly becoming a thief. But if he needs the money to buy his wife's health . . . He's the kind of bloke who'd sacrifice his code of honour for her.'

'Code of honour?' repeated Young jeeringly.

Something *you* wouldn't understand, thought Rook.

Young waited, then said: 'It ought to be easy enough to check on the uncle.'

'I reckon. So as soon as we get back to the station, start checking.'

Young was silent for a few seconds, then he said: 'Fancy retiring to Mallorca. From all accounts, you might as well choose Blackpool.'

.   .   .   .   .

Hazel met Drude at the small coffee bar just behind the high street which she had, in her over-romantic mind, come to think of as 'their' coffee bar.

'Hullo, darling,' she said, as she sat down on the bench seat. 'I'm not late, am I? Mr Queen wanted two letters done just as I was getting ready to leave.'

He stirred his coffee and felt sorry for himself because he liked women to be smart and sophisticated.

'Mr Queen's always doing that sort of thing. Glenda refuses to work for him, but she's been with the force so long that she can get away with it. If I did that I'm sure they'd fire me. Still, I suppose he's not really too bad. At least he doesn't stand by the stairs like one of the P.C.s and try to look up people's skirts.' She giggled. 'I make certain I keep near the wall, I can tell you.' She put her hand on his arm. 'There's only one person allowed to do anything like that,' she whispered.

He managed to conceal his contempt.

'Love, could we go to the flics tonight? There's a lovely picture on. Afterwards, we could go back home for some supper and you could see Mum and Dad. I so want you to meet them.'

Hard-boiled eggs and pickled onions with Mum in her curlers and Dad in his pink braces. 'I've a better idea. We'll go to Francisco where there's a dance on.'

She usually didn't argue with him because he became so annoyed, but now she said: 'I can't. I mean, not in this dress. I've been wearing it all day. . . .'

'Looks all right to me.' He realized he ought to appear more loving. 'I mean, it suits you and makes you look like a million dollars, so who's going to worry?'

The waitress, looking nearly as tired as she felt, came across and took Hazel's order.

He offered Hazel a cigarette. 'How's the work going, love, apart from the stupid bastard who made you late?'

'It's all right, but the real trouble is there's enough to do to keep six of us busy and with June on holiday there's only us three.'

'Are you still working on the bank robbery?'

'Every now and then there's a report comes through – there was one the other day as a matter of fact. But I'll tell you something!' She giggled. 'I had to type out a report today that made me blush and it's not as if I don't know what goes on, having worked there for a couple of years now. You'd never believe . . .'

'What kind of report came through, then?'

'I'm telling you, love.'

'I mean over the bank raid.'

She shrugged her shoulders. 'It was from Mr Young . . . Mary went out with him one evening and she said she spent most of it trying to make him keep his hands to himself.'

'Have they found the gunmen at last?'

'No, they don't know where they are. Sergeant Young's been checking up on three of the bank staff for something or other.'

'How d'you mean, checking up?'

'What cars they've got, whether they've bought expensive things recently – all that sort of thing.'

'Had any of 'em?'

'No. They all sounded as dull as they come.' She gazed lovingly at him. 'Not all special, like you and me.'

'I've a pal called Lever what works in the bank. Were they checking up on him? Be a lark if they was.'

'Lever? No. They were called Seebring, Hodges, and Steen. I knew a chap called Hodges once and you'll never believe this, he used to . . .'

16

Young yawned as he walked along the corridor to Rook's office. It had been a bitch of a day, mostly spent on the telephone. The D.I. was out. Young went round behind the desk and looked at all the files which had collected on it. Rook was ignoring the routine work and spending most of his time trying to trace the money from the bank job in a frantic effort to regain some credibility as a detective suitable for promotion. Sheer waste of time, thought Young. He wrote on the pad which was kept on the desk for messages. George Steen had had two sons, Silas George and Brian Harold. Silas had been born on the fifteenth of August, seventy-three years before, Brian on the twenty-first of December, sixty-six years before. Brian had died at the age of sixty-two, his wife one year later, leaving as sole issue William George. No death certificate had ever been issued for Silas George.

Old George Steen had lived in Bristowe, twelve miles from Scranton Cross, in a house now demolished. One person had been traced who remembered the family and although his recollections were very vague he said he remembered there'd been some sort of scandal over the elder son who'd left home.

So much for the D.I.'s too-convenient coincidence, thought Young, as he finished writing.

·   ·   ·   ·   ·   ·

Thomas lay on the bed and cursed the world. For well over a month now he'd been jailed up in the house, leaving it only twice, once to murder Keen, once to release his body. Ginger, Alf, and Flash, had become so bloody minded it was becoming increasingly difficult to prevent their fighting over the most absurd grievances. And the police, if Paul were to be believed, weren't getting anywhere.

Money would soon get tight. Goddamn it, he thought, something had to break soon. Eventually the splits must get something right. Why couldn't they find out which of the bank staff had made the switch?

    .   .   .   .   .

The letter arrived on the seventeenth of September, a Friday. When he came down from the bedroom and unlocked the inner door, Steen saw it on the sill of the porch which was where the postman always left the mail.

He opened the letter. It was written on headed paper. Cifret – in good English in which only a few words were misused – said that he was sorry to have to give the sad news that Señor Silas Steen had died. Mercifully, he had not suffered too much. Under his will, now being forwarded to Madrid, he left his house, its contents, and the land, together with all his capital, to his nephew, William Steen. There would, of course, be inheritance taxes to be paid (not too severe since Señor Steen was a fairly close relative) but the capital available would certainly be sufficient to meet these and there should be a reasonable sum left over. If Señor William Steen could visit the island soon it would be of great assistance since he was needed to sign certain documents.

Steen went up to their bedroom and handed Penelope the letter. 'It's from Mallorca, darling. Uncle Silas has died. He's left everything to me.'

She stared at the envelope, then at him. 'Is that . . . Is it quite certain you get the house?'

'Read what the solicitor says.'

She withdrew the letter and read it. She looked up. 'So it's actually happened. Bill, I don't know whether to laugh or cry.'

'I'd try laughing because that's less likely to bring on an attack of asthma.'

She came forward and held him tightly as she kissed him. 'It's a dream that's really coming true and I don't know I can believe it. Maybe I'll never have to go into hospital again feeling as if I'm going to choke to death, or have adrenalin injections which are like liquid fire. . . . Oh, Bill, I feel quite tight! Don't go to work today. I'll ring up and tell them you're not well. I must talk and talk. All these weeks I've been bottling things up because there was always the chance it might not happen. Now it's happened and if I don't talk, I'll explode. How am I going to learn to get my Spanish straightened out so that when I ask for butter I don't get raspberry jam? What clothes am I going to need? Does it get cold in winter? When are we off?'

'At least I can answer that last one. As soon as we possibly can be.'

'You'll have to go out first, won't you, to get everything straightened out as the solicitor suggests?'

He shook his head. 'Why? The house is empty and surely no one can stop us living in it even if all the legal ends haven't been tied up yet? Why don't we just pick up sticks and go, before the prospect starts looking too daunting?'

'But what about the bank?'

'I'm officially bound to give them a month's notice, but

143

I'm sure if I ask Wraight for an earlier release he'll give it to me, knowing the circumstances.'

'What do we do with this house?'

'We'll see the agents and arrange to put it up for sale right away. I read that the market's improving, so they should be able to sell it without too much trouble. We'll have to apply to emigrate so we can have an external account . . . At least that's one thing I can do on my own!'

'Then how soon d'you think it'll be before we go?'

'We'll leave as early in October as we possibly can. It's the end of October when you so often catch a nasty cold.'

They both knew what he really meant, but between them had grown up the habit – superstitious in origin – of never referring to the possibility of a bad asthma attack.

She walked over to the south facing window. As she stared out at the distant woods, she said: 'I wonder if the house will remember us?'

. . . . .

Rook received a telephone message that Wraight would like to see him. He cut short the work he was doing and walked from divisional H.Q. to the bank.

In his office, Wraight shook hands, then resumed his seat and stared at Rook with an aggrieved expression. He was a man who had always known exactly where his duty lay and had had no hesitation in following it. Yet now his duty lay in opposite directions. He must help the police because it was every citizen's duty to do so: he demanded allegiance from the staff and in return it was his duty to give them his loyal support.

Rook, who read the other's character accurately and

could understand the mental conflict, waited patiently.

Wraight coughed. He locked his fingers together and rested his hands on the desk. 'You asked me to inform you of any developments in connexion with William Steen's inheritance of his uncle's estate in Mallorca, Inspector.'

Rook nodded. 'That's right.'

Wraight coughed again. 'He came to me this morning and showed me a letter from a solicitor on the island. His uncle has died and left him the estate and as a result he has given in his notice. He asked me if he might be released from the contractual need to work for a further full month and I have agreed to his working for only the next fortnight.'

Rook rubbed his chin. 'What kind of a letter was it? Was it on headed notepaper?'

'Yes. And it was written in English, of course, or I certainly should not have understood a single word.'

'Did you by any chance remember the name and address of the solicitor?'

'I made a point of remembering them.' He pulled a sheet of paper to himself. 'Cifret Alvarez is the man's name – Steen was telling me that he believes all Spaniards have two surnames, although they're commonly known only by the first one. The address was fourteen, Calle de la Huerta. I'll spell that out as I'm sure I'm pronouncing it wrongly.'

Rook wrote down the name and address. 'Have you any kind of idea what the estate consists of?'

'From what Steen has told me the house isn't large, but it is more than adequate – a three hundred-year-old farm-house, built in the local kind of sandstone. There's a garden with all sorts of flowers and fruits – lemons, oranges, persimmons. I must confess I understood the entire island had long since become a concrete jungle, but he says that parts of it are still very beautiful and he's going to live in one of the beautiful ones.'

'He's very lucky. Not many people get the breaks.'

'And of those, how many have the necessary mental courage to do what he's doing?' asked Wraight shrewdly. 'He's throwing up a good career. But then if the move really helps the health of his wife, I'm sure he'll consider that a small price to pay.'

'Did he say when he's leaving England?'

'As soon as possible in October. The wet weather so often affects his wife's health.'

'What's he going to live on? Fresh air and hope?'

'There's enough capital to pay death duties and leave something over. He'll have the money from the sale of his house here, less the mortgage and overdraft repayments. And on top of that he's also hoping to sell some of his paintings. I gather there's quite an artists' colony in and around Llueyo.'

'From what I saw of his paintings I wouldn't have thought he'd earn much from them.'

'One never knows,' replied Wraight didactically. 'He says he can do landscapes which are immediately recognizable and that's what most visiting tourists want.'

'I suppose he's probably right there.' Rook closed his notebook and replaced it in his pocket. 'Well, that seems to cover everything. Thanks a lot for getting in touch with me.'

Wraight nodded.

Back at divisional H.Q., Rook telephoned London and spoke to the county liaison officer at New Scotland Yard and asked for a request to be put through to the Spanish police for a check to be made whether there was such a person as Cifret Alvarez living at fourteen, Calle de la Huerta, and if so that he be questioned concerning the death of Silas Steen.

. . . . .

Torcuato was short, even for a Mallorquin, but by way of compensation he had a thick, stocky body which spoke of considerable strength. His black, curly hair was just beginning to be threaded with grey and when he was tired nowadays his pleasantly ugly face became drawn.

He parked his rattletrap Seat 600 and walked along the Calle de la Huerta, so narrow that at this time of the day the harsh sunshine failed to reach the surface of the road. He knocked on the door of number fourteen and stepped inside, as was the custom, and when the woman with gappy teeth came into the entrance hall he said, 'Good afternoon, señora.'

'Good afternoon, señor. The señor is very busy . . .'
He interrupted her. 'Cuerpo General de Policia.'
Her expression became wary. The power of the C.I.D. had grown no less, even if they now seldom exercised it to the full.

'I want a quick word with Señor Cifret.'
'Please sit down, señor. I'll tell him you're here.'
He sat and waited, without any sense of impatience because he was an islander and time was unimportant. After a while, Cifret came out of his office with a couple to whom he spoke in English. More rich foreigners buying up the best parts of the island, Torcuato thought resentfully.

Cifret saw them out of the front door, then hurried over

147

to Torcuato and shook hands. He led the way into his untidy office. 'You'll have a cognac, señor?'

'I certainly will.'

He crossed to a pile of books and brought from behind them a half-full bottle of brandy and two glasses. He poured out the drinks and passed one glass across. 'At this time of the afternoon, a cognac is very soothing for the stomach.'

Torcuato nodded and drank. He seldom spoke when it wasn't necessary.

Cifret leaned back in his chair. 'Tell me, Señor, what brings you here?' His manner was easy, but there was a sharp, watchful expression in his eyes.

'Do you know the name of an Englishman, señor . . .' Torcuato took a piece of paper from the pocket of his lightweight jacket. 'Señor Silas Steen?' He had difficulty in pronouncing the two names.

'Señor Steen has recently died after an illness.' Cifret's thoughts were uneasy. Had he made a ghastly mistake in helping to fake the 'death' of Silas Steen? At no time had he imagined that the Cuerpo General de Policia would become interested in the case. . . .

'Where did he live?'

'In Ca'na Xema. A nice house with a beautiful garden, but one that needs a great deal of water.'

'Have you handled the matters arising from his death?'

'I have. All the papers are with Madrid now — perhaps in a few months' time they will begin to deal with them. I've written to the heir and he says he's coming very soon to live in the house.'

'What's his name?'

'William Steen.'

'Is there any money as well as the house?'

'You mean after all the taxes have been paid, and my fees? A little. Perhaps a million.'

'I'd call a million a lot of money.'

Cifret shrugged his shoulders. 'You and I would call it a fortune. But these foreigners have many, many millions.'

Torcuato finished his drink.

'Will you have another cognac?'

'Not for me. I've got to get back to the office and send a message to London.'

'What's the trouble – something to do with the will?'

'Search me.' Torcuato stood up.

Cifret decided to increase his bill to Steen by way of compensation for this extra worry.

．　　　．　　　．　　　．　　　．

Rook stared at the neatly typed report. The Spanish police confirmed that Señor Cifret Alvarez was a solicitor, living in Llueyo. He was dealing with matters arising from the death of Señor Silas Steen and the estate consisted of a house and a limited amount of capital, all of which had been left to a nephew in England, name of William Steen. Probate had not been granted, but all necessary papers were with the authorities in Madrid.

Rook dropped the report on his desk. That was that, then. Steen really was the heir to his uncle's estate and the fact that he had first heard of this possible inheritance after the bank robbery was no more than a coincidence, however fortunate. Since Steen had ended up as the only reasonable suspect who could have switched the money, it was now logical to assume that the money had not been switched. From this followed the fact that Dutch Keen's murder had had no direct connexion with the bank job.

He swore. Until now he'd always had the hope that he'd be able to trace the money and so salvage something from the case.

    .   .   .   .   .

Drude arrived at the house in Yexton as night was beginning. He parked the car in the garage and used the inside door to go through to the kitchen. From there he went into the sitting-room. Thomas, Chase, Brent, and Jenkins, were slumped in chairs, watching the television.

Thomas looked round. 'Have you got any news?' he asked.

'Yeah. But it's bad. The splits have checked Steen right out. He did have an uncle who died and left him a house and some cash. The Spanish police talked to the mouth-piece who handled the business. So Steen's legit and the splits say that's an end to it. The money wasn't switched after all and Dutch was murdered for a reason they don't know.'

Had Dutch fooled them all? wondered Thomas. Had he switched the money and hidden it and then somehow found the courage to keep quiet through all that torture? If the splits couldn't trace anyone who could have done the switch . . .

But surely his original assessment of Dutch's courage was the correct one? Ten seconds of the lighter and he'd sing, ten minutes and he'd betray his wife, daughter, mother. . . .

The others were staring at him, waiting for him to speak. The silly bastards, he thought. Goddamn it, did they expect he could perform miracles? He'd played it every way he could, so if it had closed up, it had closed up, period. But two hundred and seventy-five thousand quid couldn't just disappear. It had to be somewhere. If Dutch hadn't had the guts, the truth was that the money *had* been switched. And only a member of the bank could have switched it. But the splits had investigated and come up with the fact that everybody was as white as Persil. . . .

If the police had known for certain that the money *had* been switched, would they have had a different starting point and would it matter what was their starting point? . . . He saw that it mattered a great deal. In the one case, failure to uncover someone living richly suggested there had been no switch: in the other, this failure said that the investigations must be incomplete.

There *had* been a switch, only one of the bank staff had ever seriously been under suspicion, he'd come into money, but legitimately. . . . If one wanted to hide a fortune, didn't the really smart man hide it by turning it into legitimate money? Mightn't Steen have proved himself cleverer than the splits because they didn't know for certain there had been a switch? . . .

'So what do we do now?' demanded Brent.

'What do we do, you stupid git?' shouted Chase. 'We don't do nothing because there ain't nothing we can do.'

Jenkins swore violently.

Brent spoke to Thomas again. 'Val, what do we do?'

It infuriated him that they should rely on him totally. Left to themselves, he thought, they'd give up because they were ready to accept the police's assessment of events since it didn't occur to them that in a case like this the police could have been fooled. They now believed Dutch had had more courage than any of them had ever given him credit for and since he was dead . . .

He suddenly realized that he should be delighted, not

infuriated, at the way their minds were working. . . . He spoke slowly and bitterly. 'I reckon Ginger got it dead right. There ain't nothing more we can do.'

17

Like most Mallorquin farmhouses, Ca'na Xema was architecturally very simple and although its stone walls blended in perfectly with the drystone terracing and the mountains behind, it was functional in appearance rather than attractive. Inside, however, it had been restored and altered with considerable taste and attention to period features so that it no longer remained austere: there were high, beamed ceilings, tiled floors, a stone staircase which wound round in two tight right angles, an arched entrance into the sitting-room which had been the cowshed, and one of the two large open fireplaces still contained the stone vat in which clothes had occasionally been boiled.

Penelope loved the house from the moment she first walked into it. For her, houses always had a specific character: happy, sad, welcoming, resentful . . . Ca'na Xema was as happy as Tudor Cottage had been and in addition it was filled with calm. The spirit of *mañana*, she called it, distilled from decades of letting life flow by.

She found the Mallorquins – those who had not done business with foreigners – warm-hearted and generous and because this was her character she made friends with them quickly and effortlessly. She began to try to speak Castilian to them, despite her self-consciousness, and they helped her, correcting her whenever necessary with smiling tact. She met a number of the local English residents and discovered that among those who were rich there were just as many who were smugly confident of their own superiority as there would have been back in England, but that the majority were far more informally friendly than she had expected.

In the latter part of November she caught a cold. Within a day it was obvious it was going to be a heavy one and experience told her it must develop into asthma and bronchitis. She waited in dread for the first bubbling breaths which would herald the coming storm and she wondered if the hospitals in Palma would be as efficient as had been the general hospital in Scranton Cross. Three days later, and without a single bubbling breath, she realized the cold was fast waning. 'Bill, it's a miracle! I was so certain I was for it.' It was the first time she had ever confessed that she had been afraid.

.   .   .   .   .

The gallery was a newly built, L-shaped building just outside Llueyo. In the courtyard were various statues and inside were hung paintings by local artists, both Mallorquin and foreign. Vives's office was at the far end of the short part of the L.

He came round his desk and shook Steen's hand. 'Good morning, señor. A pleasure to meet you once more. You will have a cognac?'

'I'm afraid it's still a bit early for me.'

'You are an Englishman who waits for the sun to get

so high? We Mallorquins do not have such a custom.' He smiled. 'Sit yourself, señor, in that chair.' Vives sat behind the desk. 'The weather has been good, has it not?' He fidgeted with some promotional material on his desk: he seldom was still. 'I see that you have not brought me more of your paintings. Why is that?'

'I gave you three only the other day.'

'But I wish for many more.'

Steen smiled. 'I can't afford to paint too many!'

'Señor, that I understand! Every time you paint a picture you make yourself two thousand pesetas poorer. But now I have some news for you. An American was in here and he saw one of your paintings and bought it. So I have to give you eight thousand pesetas and I already have my two thousand.' He took a key from his pocket and unlocked the top right-hand drawer of his desk. 'Señor, I shall hang your paintings for longer instead of taking them away quickly because I think people will buy them. They have much brightness and are not too big to return to another country and remind a person of this island.'

'Perfect chocolate-box art.'

Vives stared shrewdly at Steen. 'Señor, I think you should not be so severe about your paintings. They are not great art, but people like them. Be proud of them. There are artists who live here who would be pleased to paint as well as you.'

Steen was surprised because it seemed that Vives was speaking genuinely.

'I will tell you how I feel, Señor. In your paintings is something which tells me that one day you may paint better pictures. Not great pictures, you understand? But paintings that make a person look again.'

'I certainly hope you're right.'

'I am right very often.' He finally pulled open the desk drawer and brought out a number of thousand-peseta notes, from which he counted eight. He passed these across.

Steen picked up the money. 'But now I owe you four thousand for the two remaining paintings which you'll get rid of.'

'Señor, we leave that. Perhaps I also sell them and I give you more money and you need give me nothing.'

Steen hesitated, then said: 'O.K. But take them down after a week.'

'A week only? But I would like . . .' He stopped and shrugged his shoulders. 'I will do it. But please give me some paintings I can hang for a good time.'

'I will.' Steen stood up. 'Thanks a lot.'

'I think it is me who should thank. If there are many artists like you, I am rich!'

Steen shook hands and left. He walked out into the sunshine, still hot despite its being November, and crossed to his car which was parked on the hard shoulder of the road. He sat behind the wheel and stared through the windscreen at the mountains which stretched down past Puerto Llueyo. It was ironic, he thought, that Vives should ask him to leave those two paintings since he wanted to be able to tell Penelope that he had sold all three in order to explain the two hundred and forty pounds he had just changed at a bank. Now, he would be able to account for only eight thousand pesetas – she was bound to visit the gallery within the coming week. If he became at all successful and actually sold his paintings in any number, then the whole object of the exercise would be defeated!

He started the engine, made a U-turn, and drove back towards Ca'na Xema. When he had left Penelope, she had been laughing and her tanned face had been free from strain. It was incredible to realize that it was no longer true to think of her as always a potential invalid.

He turned off the metalled surface on to the dirt track which wound round to Ca'na Xema, past fields intensively cultivated and the large, ugly house owned by a very rich American woman. In some ways, he thought, he hadn't yet become mentally acclimatized to living in Mallorca. He'd look at his watch and momentarily wonder why he wasn't hard at work at the bank, trying to explain to a bewildered customer the Bank of England's rules regarding transfer of capital: at three in the afternoon, he'd remember the need to take all the travellers' cheques and foreign currency down to the strong-room. He felt uneasy that he wasn't working – he couldn't regard his painting as work – because he'd been brought up to believe every honest man should do a full day's work. (He could appreciate the irony of this. He wasn't honest and his conscience should have been troubled by the theft, not a nagging, calvanistic fear that he was in danger of becoming a layabout).

He rounded the corner, to come in sight of the house and the orange grove below it. He could see Penelope working in the garden, weeding one of the flower beds. She was working harder than she had ever been able to do at home, yet never suffered exertion asthma. Life was miraculously good.

.   .   .   .   .

From the moment he'd decided that Steen had pulled the wool over the police's eyes, Thomas was desperately impatient to get to Mallorca, yet he knew only too well that if he were to avoid the other four becoming at all suspicious of him he had to stay and seem to share their sullen resentment at the way things had gone, their fear of a future which had to be faced penniless and in the knowledge that any informer would shop them, and their seeming inability to pull themselves together and do something constructive. It was the end of November before they finally drifted away and he was free to move.

He bought two stolen passports, unused, from a man in London who charged him five hundred pounds each. He contacted a woman he'd known a year before and offered her a thousand pounds to travel to Jersey with him as Mr and Mrs Trenton. She refused. He explained what would happen to her if she continued to refuse and now she agreed. He disguised himself as far as that was practicable, with cheek pads, a different hair parting, and his moustache (grown over the past few weeks. Chase and the others had never guessed at the real reason for this). Both he and the woman had their passport photos taken in a D.I.Y. cabinet. He took these back to the seller who impressed the photographs and the title pages with a beautiful imitation of the Foreign Office seal and stamped in the issuing dates.

He booked them on a 'Pre-Christmas fun flight' to Jersey. On their arrival he gave her a thousand pounds and her passport (which had never been asked for) and told her to get lost. Then he bought a seat on the morning scheduled flight to Paris.

From Paris he travelled by train to Marseilles. He caught another train to Nice, hitch-hiked back to Cannes. He flew from Cannes to Palma, confident that no one would ever be able to trace out his journey.

.   .   .   .   .

Every year the mayor and town council of Llueyo held, in conjunction with the Club Llueyo and the Ministry of Tourism, a painting competition. Open to all residents on the island, of any nationality, the major prize was fifty thousand pesetas. There were six different categories in which a painting could be entered and in each category there were three minor prizes. Since the six judges were five town dignitaries and a local artist who believed himself a genius it was generally agreed that if one seriously hoped to win a prize too much artistic merit was a severe handicap.

Prize giving was held in the theatre at the back of the Club Llueyo. It was customary to clap loudly and not to laugh whoever won a prize and the setting had something of the air of an English minor public school sports day.

Steen was awarded third prize for his landscape of Cala Borca.

'Bill,' said Penelope, as they left the club building and went out into the square, 'I feel as if I'd drunk a bottle of champagne.'

'That's wonderful, because now there's no need to offer you a drink.'

She smiled. 'You're going to take me out to dinner to celebrate. Seriously, though, aren't you absolutely delighted?'

'Yes, of course.'

'But you're determined not to show it? Stop being such a coward.'

'A what?'

'A coward. You always seem to get so scared of anything good happening. What's the matter? Do you think someone's going to kick you hard just to even up things.'

'I suppose in a way, I am.'

'Then forget it. There's nothing superstitious about this, Bill. Years ago I said you were good, but you wouldn't believe me. Now you've proved to everyone you're really good, so enjoy it.'

He enjoyed it, not because he'd won a prize but because he'd made her feel so proud.

The square, illuminated in honour of the festival with coloured lights, was busy: because the night was so balmy, the two cafés which overlooked it had left out tables and chairs. They sat down at one of the tables and a waiter took their orders.

They sat in silence, content to enjoy the peace which somehow was enhanced, and not destroyed, by several children who were playing a complicated and noisy game of tag at the far end of the square, by the church. A donkey cart jogged past, feet clopping, to strip away decades.

The waiter brought them two sweet red vermouths and soda.

She raised her glass. 'Here's to the day you win the big prize.'

'And have my name inscribed in gold?'

'In letters six inches high . . . Bill, one day paint the bay for me. When the water's deep blue and the mountains get lost in the heat haze. When we're old and rheumaticky and not able to get around I'll be able to look at it and remember everything. . . . Especially how you threw up your job, sold the house, and risked the future just for me.' She twisted the glass round in her fingers. 'I've somehow never been able to tell you. . . .'

He interrupted her. 'Then don't now.'

She looked directly at him, her blue eyes intense. 'But I want to.'

'I know, without your telling me.' He hated all the lies

159

he had been forced into, but he hated even more the way in which she believed his sacrifices had been so much greater than they had. Once he had sacrificed his honour, the rest had been easy.

.   .   .   .   .

The cemetery, surrounded by fields, was a kilometre beyond the outskirts of the town. It was walled, with towers on either side of the large, intricately patterned wrought-iron gates. Inside were family burial chambers, some plain in style, some rococo, some Islamic.

Thomas entered and looked around, contemptuous of such fanciful trappings for death. An elderly man, badly dressed, his back bowed and one eye clearly glass, came up to Thomas and spoke in Spanish. Thomas said in English: 'I'm looking for the grave of Silas Steen. Steen. He was English.'

The man seemed perplexed, but then he suddenly nodded. He turned and walked up a path of loose chippings to the far end of the cemetery where, against the wall, was a completely plain burial chamber. There were small 'shelves' outside and on one of these were roses in a glass vase and a plastic-covered, black-edged card which read: 'Silas Steen, born 15 August 1904. Died aged 73. R.I.P.'

He'd so convinced himself that the death had been faked that now he knew both bewilderment and an impotent anger in discovering it had not. He cursed Silas Steen for having lived and died.

The man spoke and Thomas gave him a fifty-peseta piece to shut him up. And it was only as the man shuffled off that it belatedly occurred to Thomas that a clever man who 'killed' an uncle so he could be left with a house would surely go one step further and arrange for a grave. After all, a grave was the final proof of death. Or was it?

. . . . .

That night, Thomas broke into the cemetery. The burial chamber at the far end was locked, but the lock was of simple construction and he forced it within a minute. Inside were a number of 'gratings', on three of which were coffins. One of the coffins was clearly new. He unscrewed the lid and found it was filled with earth.

18

Ca'na Xema stood on the dying slopes of a mountain and behind the house there was a three-hundred-metre strip of maquis scrub. Trees climbed a little way up the mountainside, then it rose more precipitously and its surface held only pockets of grass, bushes, or an occasional stunted pine.

Thomas parked the rented Seat 600 in one of the dirt lanes and walked up the rising road which led into a valley. When he'd gone far enough he turned off and climbed the dry-stone wall, which carried the small aqueduct from a spring in the valley down to the farms, and carried on up the mountainside until he had a good view of the immediate countryside. He sat, half hidden by a spurge bush which was growing out of a crack in the rock, unslung a pair of field glasses, and studied Ca'na Xema and its surrounding land.

From his point of view, the house was conveniently situated. Although not isolated in the strictest sense, the nearest house was over four hundred metres away: beyond screaming distance, he thought with twisted amusement. He traced out the electricity wires, but could see no telephone ones: since no wires were put underground outside the towns, he could be certain the house was not on the phone. He checked the approach. Would Steen be scared of reprisals for stealing the money and therefore be prepared for them? No, he decided. Although Steen was clever, he was a civilian and civilians didn't understand. If Steen had ever thought about it, he'd merely have imagined that after their escape the bank robbers would have resignedly shrugged their shoulders over the loss of the money.

Thomas watched the wife begin to prune a rose. He hoped for her sake that Steen still had most of the money ready to hand.

.   .   .   '   .   .

Rook was preparing to leave his office on what was a typical December night – the day-long drizzle had turned to rain and the cold east wind hinted at sleet – when the telephone rang. He briefly wondered whether to ignore it, but his strict sense of duty forced him to reach out and pick up the receiver. 'D.I.'

'Detective Sergeant Trubshawe, sir, Barrackton police. I thought you'd want to know that we picked Jenkins up this morning after an abortive smash-and-grab job.'

'Flash Jenkins?'

'That's him.'

Rook, suddenly no longer feeling tired and worn out, sat down on the edge of the desk. 'What kind of news has he got for us?'

'Precious little. We got him talking and he says the bank money just vanished and none of 'em has the slightest idea where it vanished to.'

'Surely to God someone has.'

'He swears not. He's skint and, as he said, they wouldn't have split up and written the money off as a dead loss if anyone knew anything about it. . . . He also gave us one bit of news you're going to like even less.'

'What?'

Trubshawe spoke with great care. 'They were trying every way they could to trace the money and one of the ways was to make direct contact with someone in your force for information on whether you'd any idea who'd got the money. If you had had, they'd have tried to move in first.'

Rook gripped the receiver tightly. 'Who was their informant?'

'He doesn't know her name, but it was a woman. He won't say why he's so certain. Nor will he name the fifth member of the mob.'

For the moment, Rook didn't give a damn about the fifth bank robber. A traitor? Instinctively he identified her as one of the civilian employees, solely on the grounds that by his standards it was impossible any member of the force could be a traitor. He'd get her, he thought harshly.

'We've had to charge Jenkins on the smash-and-grab, but you'd probably like to come up and question him?'

'Yes.' There were rules about the interrogation of a

man in custody and after he'd been charged, but a seasoned detective knew a way round most of them.

'My D.I. says if you'll just give us an arrival time, we'll lay everything on for you. He can give you a bed if that'll help and your expenses are being cut back anything like ours are.'

'Tell him thanks a lot. I'll check up things my end and then ring you back and let you know my plans.'

After replacing the receiver, Rook drummed on the desk with his fingers. If a member of the bank mob had no idea where the money had gone, what had happened to it? Had one of the gang swindled the others – a possibility which had not arisen before? Had Dutch Keen made the switch and salted the money away and somehow found the courage to take the secret of its whereabouts with him? Had Steen worked the switch and then covered his tracks far more cleverly than had been considered possible? Each possibility must be checked out. . . .

.   .   .   .   .

Thomas drove up the track and parked the Seat under the spreading branches of an algarroba tree. The night was as yet moonless and the car would be hidden unless a direct light was shone on it. He climbed out and checked the contents of his pockets: a .25 Walther with full magazine, a cosh, a gas-filled lighter, a roll of broad adhesive tape, a torch, a small tube of very strong adhesive, and a square of mutton cloth.

He switched on his torch and walked through the maquis scrub, swearing when he inadvertently collided with a small prickly pear cactus. He found the water channel which he had earlier noted and followed this along the tops of dry-stone walls to the estanqui it fed.

From here the house was just discernible as a black mass unbroken by any light inside. He went down the steps by the side of the estanqui, which abutted one of the dry-stone walls, along a dirt path, and reached the patio.

He stood still, checking the sounds. Nearby a dog was barking and further away another picked up the call: as almost every field had a dog chained up at the entrance, supposedly to guard the field, no one took any notice of their barking, which was virtually constant. There was the hum of very late traffic on the Llueyo–Puerto Llueyo road. A light wind was moving the leaves of trees.

He crossed the patio. The front door was glass panelled for the top half: he tried the handle, but it was locked. He smeared the adhesive over the pane of glass nearest to the door handle and stuck the mutton cloth down on the adhesive. After allowing five minutes for the adhesive to set, he used the cosh to smash the glass. The noise was muted and although the glass was shattered, not a single slither fell. When he pulled the mutton cloth it brought with it much of the glass and the remainder he was easily able to work free. He reached inside and unlocked the door, entered.

He stood in the hall and again checked the sounds about him. There was none.

He switched on his torch, saw the stairs and crossed to them. They took him up to the solar, an oblong space now not used and off which were three doors, the middle one of which was ajar to show that this led into a bath-room. He listened at the left-hand door and after a while heard a rustle of movement which was almost certainly caused by a sleeper turning over.

He took the automatic from his pocket after trans-ferring the torch to his left hand, pushed down the handle of the door, kicked the door open and stepped inside.

They slept in a double bed, Penelope on the left-hand side. The noise of the door's opening had half woken her and she stirred, but Steen appeared to be still sleeping soundly.

She moved a couple of times, reached up and scratched the side of her head, then opened her eyes. Bewilderment gave way to terror. She grabbed Steen and shook him.

'Switch the light on, lady,' said Thomas.

She opened her mouth.

'Don't scream. It ain't no use.'

Steen had woken. For a second he could not understand what he'd woken to, then he threw back the bedclothes.

Thomas brought the automatic forward so that it was clearly visible in the torchlight. 'Cool it.'

Steen became still, his left leg half over the side of the bed.

'Switch on the light,' ordered Thomas, for the second time.

With a small whimper of fear, Penelope reached to her right and switched on a bedside light.

'Both of you turn over on to your fronts.'

It was obvious that Steen was judging the distance between himself and Thomas. Thomas moved forward to the side of the bed and held the muzzle of the automatic a foot away from Penelope's head. He dropped the torch on to the bed and used his left hand to rip back the bedclothes. Automatically, she reached down to adjust her nightdress. 'You can forget it, lady, I'm not after that . . . Turn over, or I'm pulling the trigger.'

She turned over. Steen hesitated, looked at the gun still close to her head, and also turned over.

'Both of you cross your ankles and put your hands behind your backs.'

They did as he ordered. 'Please, what do you want?' she asked, in a trembling voice.

He secured her wrists and ankles with adhesive tape, moved round the bed and tied up Steen. He rolled Steen over on to his back.

'We've nothing here . . .' began Steen.

'You've two hundred and seventy-five thousand quid. Or what's left of it.'

'We've nothing like that,' said Penelope, trying desperately to convince him. 'We've only a very little money. Our name's Steen . . .'

'I know that, lady. And I know that your husband lifted two hundred and seventy-five grand by switching the money in the suitcase in the bank.'

'He's never stolen anything in his life.'

'Yeah? So where did this house come from?'

'His uncle died and left it to us.'

'No ways, lady.'

'But I promise you. I've put flowers by the grave . . .'

'Sure, there's a grave for Silas Steen. Only there ain't no body in the coffin.'

She was now almost as bewildered as she was scared.

Steen spoke hoarsely. 'I swear my uncle left me this place. . . .'

Thomas shrugged his shoulders. 'Don't you understand nothing?' He crossed to the chair on which Steen had folded his clothes and with his left hand picked up the shirt and pair of pants. 'Open your mouth.' Steen kept his mouth shut. Thomas swept his right hand downwards to slam the butt of the automatic into Steen's cheekbone and as Steen cried out the pants were jammed into his mouth. Thomas used the shirt to tie the pants in place. He gagged Penelope with her clothes.

He returned to the right-hand side of the bed. 'Listen,'

he said in an unemotional voice, 'I want that money. I ain't interested in anything else. So tell me where it is and save yourself a lot of trouble.'

Steen shook his head.

Thomas put the automatic down on the bedside table and brought the gas lighter out of his pocket. He flicked it open and adjusted the flame until it was an inch high. 'Don't be a mug all the way.' He waited but Steen merely stared at him. 'O.K. When you want to talk, nod.'

He dragged Steen to the edge of the bed. He brought the flame up to the flesh.

At first, Steen found the pain bearable. Indeed, in a strange, crazy way, he almost welcomed it. He had stolen and betrayed his code of honour and by the terms of that code should have been punished. Instead, he had prospered. So, the prosperity for which he had not paid in any coin had frightened him. Now he was paying, in a strange coin, true, but he was paying and the score would be evened.

The pain grew until it became so obscene that it seemed impossible he could ever have welcomed it. It squeezed his mind, to become unendurable. He nodded convulsively.

Thomas shut the lighter and ungagged him. 'Where is it?'

Through the mists of agony, mercifully easing, he became aware that Penelope was sobbing violently.

Impatient, Thomas flicked open the lighter again.

'In a suitcase. In the other bedroom. In the cupboard.'

Thomas went through to the second bedroom — equipped as a studio — and in the small cupboard he found three suitcases, one of which was heavy and locked. He ripped it open with his knife. The money was inside, most of the notes still in their original brown wrappers. He made a very quick count and put the total at around two hundred and thirty thousand pounds – a hundred and twenty thousand more than he would have received under the original shareout. He smiled sardonically. Since there was no way of quickly getting back the money Steen had spent on the house, he might as well be left to enjoy it: after all, it wasn't often that the mugs of the world had the chance to come out on the right side of things.

. . . . .

Finally convinced Thomas had gone, Steen used his teeth to free Penelope's hands. She tore loose the gag and the tapes from her ankles and then, tears flooding her cheeks, freed him and examined and treated the burn on his side.

Later, after she had dressed the burn and given him aspirins, he lay on the bed with her in his arms and listened to her asking again and again, why? Thomas might have killed him: she'd thought he was being killed: she'd seen him writhing in agony and her mind had been crucified: Oh God, why had he ever risked such terror?

Would she eventually be able to understand? he wondered dully.

The pain flared up again, despite the aspirins. It was incredible that such agony could come from so small a burn: it was only about three inches long and was not deep.

She suddenly kissed him, frantic for emotional proof that he was all right.

What of the future? he wondered. Now they had little money. How long could they continue to live in the sunshine? Did they sell the house and live on the proceeds for as long as those lasted?

His thoughts were suddenly overtaken by the shocked realization that since Thomas knew it was he who had switched and finally stolen the money, he would only remain free as long as Thomas did.

19

Thomas, a man who thoroughly enjoyed the luxuries of life, leased a penthouse flat in a building overlooking the sea in Estopella, on Rosas Bay, close to the French border. Three days after signing the lease in the name of Trenton, he met Veronica Armstrong. A very attractive brunette, tall and fashionably slim, she had been on the coast for the past three years and reckoned to know her way around, but only after living with him for quite a time did she finally realize that compared to him she was a babe-in-arms. By then, she was in love with him.

One morning in early March she stood in the centre of the long sitting-room, which faced the sea, and spoke far more petulantly than she had intended. 'But why can't I come with you?'

He spoke with patience. 'Like I told you, I'm making the journey solo.'

'Yes, but why . . . ?'

'Leave it.'

'Suppose I get fed up with being on my own and clear off?'

'I'll investigate that neat little red-head we saw at the pub.'

'You bastard.'

He laughed.

'Why d'you keep going off? Where d'you go?' she asked, knowing it could prove to be a painful mistake to keep pressing him, yet unable to stop.

He shrugged his shoulders.

She went across to the settee in which he was sprawled and kissed him as she pressed her body against his. He ran his hand under her short skirt and soon she was moaning gently at the back of her throat.

He stood up. 'I'll be off then. Don't do nothing I wouldn't.' He left, without a backwards glance.

She cried tears of anger, frustration, and bitterness. The bastard had been laughing at her from the beginning. . . . She'd leave him and find someone else to flaunt in his face. But she knew that emotionally she couldn't do that, physically she didn't dare.

She crossed to the small cocktail cabinet and poured out a very strong gin and sweet red vermouth, returned to the large picture window. A strong southerly wind was driving the waves up high on to the wide sand. A couple, hand in hand, laughing as odd drops of spray stung their faces, walked along the edge of the sand. Honeymooners, she thought with contempt, trying to hide from herself her sense of envy.

She finished the drink and poured herself another. She wanted to get tight: so stinking tight that she could forget the past and ignore the future. Forget the three years of moving from man to man because she hadn't the courage to leave the life of *mañana* and return to England, ignore the possibility that one day there might not be a man willing to pick up the tabs.

171

Where in the hell did Val keep going? France? She'd once seen him check his passport before leaving. He'd be away all day and not return until late at night or maybe early next morning. After one such trip he'd drunk so much she'd dared to question him at length about where he'd been. His final answer had been the flat of his hand across her mouth.

She had a third and a fourth drink and began to feel very sorry for herself. Why couldn't he have taken her with him? Why was it – she wondered over a fifth drink – that half an hour before leaving the flat he'd gone into one of the spare bedrooms? There wasn't, as far as she knew, anything in there but some suitcases and he'd not taken one of those with him. She remembered how she'd wandered into that room soon after moving into the flat and he'd ordered her out in a way that had her running. Was there something in the cases to explain his movements?

The door of the bedroom was locked. She had had enough to drink to find that a challenge and not a warning. The locks of flats – even luxury flats – were not usually very complicated and it occurred to her that a key from one of the other doors might open this one. The second bathroom key, with a little persuasion, did so.

As expected, the bedroom was empty of anything but furniture and the suitcases. Just for a moment she became too scared to go on, but then the alcohol restored her courage. She checked the suitcases. Four were empty, the fifth one was heavy and locked.

After a moment, she remembered the key-ring Val normally wore on his trousers and which she hadn't seen on the freshly laundered pair he'd had on when he left. She went through to their bedroom and checked the trousers which had been left folded on a chair: the key ring was attached to them.

Back in the bedroom she unlocked the suitcase and opened it, to discover it was filled with English money. Amazed, she picked up some of the loose notes and crinkled them in her fingers. However much was there in the case? If that were hers, she'd never again have to be scared about the future.

She picked up a bundle of twenty-pound notes. She didn't know how much was in that bundle, but it must total many, many times as much as she'd ever before held in her hands. Yet he was always refusing to buy her things. . . . He deserved to 'lose' some of it . . . But God in heaven, if ever he discovered what she'd done! Yet with so much money could he ever know that just a few notes were missing?

From the middle of the bundle she pulled out five twenty-pound notes. If she changed the money into pesetas right away he never could discover anything.

.   .   .   .   .

Rook spoke wearily over the telephone to the county liaison officer. 'Have you tried again to tickle up the Spanish police to get them to check up on Steen?'

'Cyril, no word of a lie I've been on to them so often the phone bill's going to wreck our budget.'

'Then what in the name of hell are they doing? It's weeks since I made the first request.'

'I'd say the trouble is that they've made the enquiries once and now they're taking the fresh request as a reflection on their efficiency.'

'Haven't you told them . . .'

'I've soft-soaped them in words of one syllable.'

'Stick a ton of dynamite under their tails.'

'Can't you get the chief constable to grant a priority signal? That would get quicker action.'

What chance was there of that, thought Rook bitterly, when the expenses of the case were already far too high? And now there were dozens of other cases, of much more immediate priority in the chief constable's judgement since the bank job was history. 'There's not a hope of that, Steve. There must be some way of waking them up.'

'I'll go on trying and I suppose eventually they'll come down off their high horse and have a second check on the death of Silas Steen. But until that happens, Cyril, you're just going to have to hold your horses.'

'You can take all those bloody horses. . . . All right. Take no notice of me, I'm just an old man who gets too excited.'

Rook said goodbye. As he replaced the receiver, Young came into the room. 'There's a bit of news fresh in from Spain.'

'Yeah,' said Rook sourly. 'I've just heard it. There is no news.'

Young stared blankly at him.

'Forget it.'

'Forget what?'

'Forget whatever it is you're to forget.'

Young shrugged his shoulders. 'D'you know a place called Estopella?'

'No.'

'It's a tourist development on the Costa Brava, up near the French border.' Young sat down on the edge of the desk. 'Originally it was a marsh and they've drained that and dug a load of canals. If you've got a yacht . . .'

'Which I haven't.'

'We can't all be rich . . . Five twenties from the bank job have turned up there.'

Rook silently whistled. 'Do we know who?'

'A woman called Veronica Armstrong. The police have her passport number from when she changed the money at the bank.'

'Any history on her?'

'We're running her name through Records now.'

'I wonder . . .' Rook became silent. It seemed to be defying the fates to hope that they were finally closing in on the money.

* * * * *

Vives had been about to open a drawer and bring out a bottle of brandy, but he checked himself and leaned back in the chair in his office as he looked again at the three paintings which Steen had leant against the far wall: a fourth one had been left, facing away from the desk, by the chair. 'Señor, I do not understand. Are these paintings not to be the same? I will hang them and you will pay me?'

'No, not exactly. You see, things have unfortunately changed and I can't afford to do it like that any more. I was hoping you'd handle them as an ordinary commercial transaction? You said you were beginning to sell them.'

Vives scratched the side of his face. 'Señor, I . . . How shall I speak? I must be honest.' It was an unfortunate choice of words because it was doubtful if Vives could be wholly honest. 'I sell two of your paintings because they are O.K. But these . . . these, señor, are not O.K. If I hang them . . . They do not help me or you.'

Bitterly, Steen reflected that Vives was right. Over the past few weeks he had suffered a sense of utter despair and this had been transferred to these paintings so that instead of being bright and sunny, fair substitutes for ability, they were gloomy and completely amateurish.

He tried hard to appear unaffected by the decision. 'Thanks for looking at them, anyway.' He walked to the wall and collected up the paintings.

'Señor, there is one you have not shown.'

'It's one I did in a different style. . . . I don't think it'll be any good as these three aren't.'

'But permit me to look.'

Reluctantly, because he was not a man who could take failure lightly or could easily sell himself, he turned the fourth painting round. It was not chocolate-box art. In the foreground was the old fisherman mending his nets and in the background was the harbour: the fisherman was not painted sympathetically – on his face was the look of a man who had cause to know how vicious the world could become, who had been beaten almost into submission yet who had found one last spark of resistance and so fought back.

Vives stared at the painting. 'That I hang! And that I sell for much pesetas. It is not Goya, but it is good. The face disturbs me. Señor, paint more like that and together we will make much money.' He pulled open the drawer and brought out the bottle of brandy and two glasses.

Strangely, Steen knew no sudden flash of renewed hope. He just tiredly wondered by what paradox success could spring out of failure? For days before painting that picture he'd tried to get Penelope to understand his state of mind when he'd stolen the money in the strong-room and for days she'd struggled to understand and had failed. How had he ever dared risk so much? Thomas could have killed him. Didn't he understand that his life and freedom were more precious by far to her than a few asthmatic attacks? Didn't she, he'd cried in return, realize that her health was ten times paramount? In the end, baffled, upset because it seemed his sacrifices were resented when he might have expected them to be appreciated, he'd begun this painting.

Vives poured out two drinks. He passed one glass across.

.   .   .   .   .

They first learned the news when she read it out from the local English speaking newspaper, the *Majorca Daily Bulletin*. A second of the robbers from the siege in the Scranton Cross bank, Val Thomas, had been recaptured in Estopella, on the Peninsula.

She said, before looking up, 'It also reports that a lot of the money was recovered.' Then she looked up and when she saw his expression she drew in her breath. 'Bill . . . Bill, what's the matter?'

He struggled to regain his composure. 'Nothing.'

'Don't be stupid . . . Oh!' Her voice dropped to a whisper. 'It's me who's being stupid. He's going to tell the police about you.'

'He won't do that.'

'But if the police . . .'

'He'll keep his mouth shut.'

'You . . . you really think he will?'

'Yes,' he lied.

'Thank God!' she murmured, knowing he was lying yet just for a moment wanting him to believe that she didn't.

20

The taxi drew up outside the main gates of Alcubierrno prison and Rook climbed out. He buttoned up his mackintosh against the rain and wondered, as he paid the driver, where the Mediterranean climate had gone to? Didn't the holiday posters promise blue skies and bikini-clad women the year round?

A warder, pistol in holster at his hip, opened the small door to the side of the much larger ones and Rook said in English that he had an appointment at the prison with Superior Chief Baldo. At the third repetition of the name the guard understood and waved him in.

In design, the prison resembled most other old ones that Rook had ever visited, but the atmosphere was noticeably different – prisoners doubled everywhere and the guards, all armed, were coldly watchful and clearly there was none of the backchat which now went on in English prisons.

He was escorted to the nearest administrative building and shown into a ground floor room sparsely furnished and painted in the dull, depressing brown which seemed to be favoured by institutions throughout the world. Left on his own, he leafed through a couple of the magazines that were on the glass-topped table, but the words were meaningless and the photos almost all of people he'd never heard of. He sat back and smoked and watched the drips trickle down to the floor from his mackintosh, which he'd hung on the elaborate coat-stand.

Superior Chief Baldo was a small, bouncy man, balding and yet with a luxuriant moustache. He shook hands vigorously and said twice, in passable English, that he was honoured to be meeting a distinguished detective from the world famous Scotland Yard. Rook tried to explain the difference between the Metropolitan and county police forces, but gave up when Baldo said yes he understood and for a third time spoke glowingly of the world-wide reputation of Scotland Yard.

Coffee was brought to them. Prison coffee was never good, Baldo said, but usually it was hot and on a day inspired by the devil it was good to drink something hot. Was it raining in England? Rook said it had been early that morning. Baldo talked about a visit he had made to England five years before in July when it had rained on every day – it was no wonder the English were such great eaters of roast beef.

Twenty minutes later, when Rook was feeling so tired that he kept half nodding off, Baldo finally said that they would now interview the prisoner. They left the administrative building and crossed through the rain to the nearest cell-block. On the ground floor, close by one of the watch points manned by an armed guard, was the interview room. Baldo called out an order to the guard before they entered and they had been seated only a couple of minutes when Thomas, handcuffed, was brought in. Baldo spoke in Spanish and the guard left: they heard him take up position outside.

'You'll remember me. I'm Detective Inspector Rook,' said Rook.

Thomas smiled crookedly. 'And there was me thinking you was Santa Claus, come with a pardon.'

'You're aware that in the flat you were renting in Estopella the police found a large sum of money and that the numbers of the twenty pound notes show these came from the bank in Scranton Cross where you were arrested?'

'I'm dead ignorant. I don't know nothing.'

179

'The prisoner will be polite and show respect,' said Balbo sharply.

Thomas looked at him with open hatred.

'How did you get that money out of the bank?' asked Rook.

Thomas stared through the barred window at the cheerless scene beyond. Nothing would be more satisfying than to shop Steen, to send him to the nick. But for Steen, he'd not have ended up in Estopella and met that bitch Veronica who'd got tight enough to lift a hundred in twenties and change them openly at a bank in her own name . . . But to shop Steen was to tell the splits that the money had not been in the suitcase Dutch Keen had withdrawn from the bank and when they knew that they would know the motive for Dutch's torture and murder. The bank job and the jail break were good for fifteen years, the sentences to run concurrently, but Dutch's murder was a cert for a lifer – with no remission.

He spoke in a toneless voice. 'I did a deal with Dutch.'

'When? You were locked up in the bank until we grabbed you.'

'I reckoned you'd have a tap on the phone so I sent a note out with the bloke who skipped the bank. This bloke's a bit dumb and he's easy to pressure, so he never thought of opening the note to see what it was about.'

'And what was it about?'

'I asked Dutch if he wanted one grand for the job, or preferred the sound of twenty. He always was a greedy bastard. So he agreed to do the switch.'

'You decided to swindle your own mob?'

'Why get excited? I'm not a boy scout.'

'You're certainly not that,' said Rook, with grim contempt. 'How did he work it?'

'Dead easy. I'd stowed some sealing-wax and twine

from the strong-room under the money. Dutch picked up the suitcase and took off. He used a hot knife to slice through the seals, leaving the impression, cut the twine, took out the money, repacked the case with papers, tied it up like it was, put a bit of sealing-wax on each knot and stuck the tops of the old seals back on. Then he handed the case over. No one noticed nothing when we opened up – they was all too eager to get a look at the money to check the seals that closely.'

'So Dutch had two hundred and seventy-five thousand?'

'S'right.'

'And he got a rush of blood to the head and took off, meaning to leave you in the cold? You had other ideas and grabbed hold of him, put the screws on, and forced him to tell you where the money was?'

'Give over. D'you think me mug enough to tell you all this if that's the way it went? Knowing I'd be for a murder rap?'

'What then?'

'I don't know for certain, any more'n you – and you're the clever one. But I can guess. He must've shouted loud and clear, mustn't he, about being rich and having twenty grand? Someone got a liking for that twenty grand and screwed the information out of him.'

'Who?'

'I'm no grasser.'

'But you swindled your own mob.'

'Yeah. But that was between friends, wasn't it?'

.   .   .   .   .

One of the first things Rook did on his return to Scranton Cross was to telephone the county liaison officer.

'Look, Cyril,' said the other wearily, 'I've been on to

Spain so often I'm beginning to speak Spanish. *Un vino tinto, pronto*. They're always very polite and promise to initiate the investigations immediately, but . . .'

'It's all right, you can cancel the request.'

'That's great! That's dead lovely! I spend days pleading, begging, cajoling, trying to blast some life into them and you . . .'

Rook ceased to listen. He wondered how the chief constable regarded the bank job now that so much of the money had been recovered?

. . . . .

An early, moist spring had brought out the wild flowers in profusion on the mountains and plain of Mallorca and everywhere there was colour.

Careless of all the beauty, Steen drove down to Puerto Llueyo and parked in front of a newsagent. He went inside and the woman behind the counter smiled at him and searched for his paper among the pile reserved for foreign residents. She handed it to him and he paid her thirty pesetas. He couldn't really afford that much, especially when the pound was suffering a very bad attack of hiccups, but he had to know what was happening back in England.

In the car he skimmed the front page, then turned over to the second and immediately saw a poor photograph of Thomas. A pulse in his throat began to hammer. For some reason beyond guessing at, Thomas had not yet told the police the full truth, but if his trial had started then the truth must come out. Steen, not yet reading the text, lowered the paper and looked along the short stretch of road to the harbour. Yachts rode at their berths and behind them, on the far side of the bay, the mountains rose up into the blue sky: a scene of beauty. His mind travelled. Penelope had had only one severe attack of asthma and bronchitis during the winter, an attack that had been controlled solely by antibiotics. No hospitalization. But now what? Accepting the need to face facts, he'd tried to persuade her to stay on the island for as long as the money lasted after he'd been extradited back to England, but she'd refused to consider the idea. The prison would have visiting hours and unless she were too ill she would be there. . . . He looked away from the harbour and back at the paper. He read, at first not really understanding because he was not concentrating. Then, a sentence jerked his attention and he went back to the beginning of the article and re-read it and finally understood that at the trail Thomas had lied to the police about what had happened to the money in the suitcase in the bank.

He dropped the paper on to the steering wheel and once more stared out at the harbour. He wanted to shout with joy, to laugh without restraint, but being English he merely put the paper on the other seat, started the engine, and drove away from the kerb. He decided to buy a bottle of champagne at the supermarket so that he and Penelope could drink a toast. To Val Thomas who in the final event had done all he could to make amends for the pain and suffering he had caused in the past.

Thomas would have been sourly amused by that.

*If you have enjoyed this book, you might
wish to join the Walker British Mystery Society*

*For information, please send a postcard or
letter to:*

Paperback Mystery Editor

**Walker & Company
720 Fifth Avenue
New York, NY 10019**